THE SUPERVILLAIN HANDBOOK

Good (Bad) Praise for *The Supervillain Handbook*

"Contained within the pages of *The Supervillain Handbook* is an easy-to-follow blueprint for villainy and world domination. If it should fall into the wrong hands, it could threaten the very foundations of our society. Those of us who value decency and the rule of law must rush out and purchase every copy we find! Every copy we buy is a copy that won't end up in the clutches of some aspiring supervillain."
—Chris Roberson, former writer of *Superman*

"At long last, everything YOU or your loved ones need to give themselves over wholeheartedly to the meaningful and lasting pursuit of villainy has been recorded in these pages. Had I this book in high school, you'd be wearing a grey uniform right now and your hair would be shaved into a, like, reverse-monk sort of thing I had figured out, as, if I had this book in high school, you would all be my minions and the world would be my playground. My loss is YOUR gain. Hail King Oblivion!"
—Matt Fraction, writer of *Iron Man* and *Thor*

"A darkly clever book invaluable to the supervillain community. And I'm not just saying that because the author's hyperphotonic deathray is pointed at my loved ones."
—Mark Waid, writer of *Daredevil*, and formerly *The Fantastic Four, The Flash*, and *Captain America*

"This book is going to elevate otherwise common criminals like CEOs and hedge fund managers into full-on world menaces—oh wait, they already are. At least now they'll know how to rock a cape and boots though, so well done! Carry on."
—Jeff Parker, author of the supervillain team book, *Thunderbolts*

THE SUPERVILLAIN HANDBOOK

The Ultimate How-to Guide to Destruction and Mayhem

King Oblivion, Ph.D.
Founder, the International Society of Supervillains
(As told to Matt D. Wilson)
Illustrated by Adam Wallenta

Skyhorse Publishing

Skyhorse Publishing books may be purchased in bulk at special discounts for
sales promotion, corporate gifts, fund-raising, or educational purposes. Special
editions can also be created to specifications. For details, contact the Special Sales
Department, Skyhorse Publishing, 307 West 36th Street,
11th Floor, New York, NY 10018 or info@skyhorsepublishing.com.

Skyhorse® and Skyhorse Publishing® are registered trademarks of Skyhorse
Publishing, Inc. ®, a Delaware corporation.

www.skyhorsepublishing.com

10 9 8 7 6 5 4 3 2

Library of Congress Cataloging-in-Publication Data

The supervillain handbook : the ultimate how-to guide to destruction
and mayhem / King Oblivion, Ph.D., founder, the International Society of
Supervillains (as told to Matt D. Wilson).
    p. cm.
  ISBN 978-1-61608-711-1 (pbk. : alk. paper)
1. Criminals—Humor. 2. Villains in literature. 3. Superheroes—Humor.
4. Comic books, strips, etc. I. Wilson, Matt D.
  PN6231.C73S87 2012
  818'.607—dc23
                        2011045687

Printed in China

For Vic von Doom, my hero (villain)

Pathetic fools! You dare to think that the tome you now hold is anything but the key to your impending doom? Do you not understand the severity and brilliance of the trap you have set for yourself by purchasing and reading a volume by the very villains who hunger for your demise? Have you no idea that the money you have so frivolously spent on these pages will inevitably fund worldwide chaos?

You shall soon pay for your insolence! You shall soon learn from your mistakes! But not before this conveniently packaged, essential villain's how-to guide shall bring about your complete destruction!

MWA-HA-HA-HA-HA-HA-HA-HA-HA!

* * *

Got you, didn't I?

I'm King Oblivion, Ph.D., founder and overlord of the International Society of Supervillains (ISS). You've made the right (wrong) choice in picking up *The Supervillain Handbook,* the best and only resource for cads, scoundrels, ne'er-do-wells, and heels looking to go professional. The chilling mini-monologue I just used to kick off this guide is only a taste of what you might soon be able to achieve if you decide to enter the competitive, yet, rewarding world of supervillainy.

People everywhere are looking for viable alternatives to the average, ho-hum job market and its constant cycle of hirings and firings, pay cuts, and pension reforms. Super-villainy offers just that. Adventure! Maniacal laughter! Dynamic outfits! Death rays! Underwater lairs! A sensible retirement plan! Punching! All these things are within your grasp.

But it isn't all just fun and torture. There's a lot of preparation involved, and creating mass hysteria and fear for a living isn't for everyone. Still, being a career scoundrel can be the most satisfying work in the world, if you're up to it.

If this sounds like what you're looking for in a career, then read on, recruit, and be prepared to enter the world of wrong, wrathful wickedness!

CONTENTS

Prologue

All You Need to Know About the International Society of Supervillains

When you picked up this book for the first time and felt its overwhelming power over you, its undeniable magnetic pull daring you to thumb through its pages and glance through its passages, you likely noticed the many mentions of the International Society of Supervillains in the text and wondered, "What the hell is that all about? And why's the abbreviation the same as the International Space Station's?" That's good (bad), because our goal all along has been to operate just under the surface of public notice, doing evil without wide public knowledge (the one obvious exception being when we stupidly bribed all those space agency officials for the naming rights to the International Space Station).

I know you had these questions, because I pulled out my patented Psychomonitor thought-reading device to get a sense of the questions people buying and/or reading this book have. To answer the question that just popped into your head: the ISS attorney, The Litigatron, says reading this sentence equals compliance with Psychomonitor use, and it's not like I'd care if it were legal anyway, so there.

For a timeline of our exploits, I suggest you read through the entirety of this book to get to the history of the ISS, near the back. (No skipping ahead. You should be aware that we have included special traps to spring on readers who skip ahead and try to get the advance supervillainy tips before reading about the basic stuff. Don't be gettin' presumptuous all in here, for serious.)

If you absolutely must know some juicy information about the worldwide evil organization I head because you're some kind of paranoid maniac who feels like you have to see some sort of proof of expertise before you read an entire guidebook written by someone claiming to be an expert—which makes you a rare reader in the self-help genre, and we've got the research to back that up—then, fine; I'll give you some of the highlights, Mr. I-Won't-Blindly-Believe-Anything-Anyone-Tells-Me-So-I'm-Gonna-Make-It-Hard-For-Everyone. But you should realize that you're delaying gratification for all the other readers who just want to find out how to tie teenage do-gooders to giant piano strings.

Statistics

- The ISS has been creating worldwide chaos for over fifty years. Things got a little shaky in the 1990s, when we all mysteriously lost our feet in a freak accident, but they've picked back up in the last decade or so.
- Our membership has grown 100-fold since our founding in the early 1960s. Much like the members of the Screen Actors Guild, most card-carrying villains work as waiters while awaiting their big break. (And we know they'll get there soon! Keep reaching for the moonbases, folks!) This is the cause of the recent poison-gas-and-also-urine-in-food trend in most fine dining establishments.
- At least thirty percent of the people who have turned to villainy and/or henchmandom in the past fifty years have done so voluntarily.

- Supervillainy is a $900,000,000,000,000,000,000,000,000,0 00,000,000,000,000,000 per year business. Most of that money comes directly to the CEO (me). Many of you are thinking, "That income disparity is terrible!" To which I reply, "Supervillains."
- There are exactly zero legitimate superheroes still in existence. Comic books and movies would have you believe that superheroes are still a big deal, but they are terrible propaganda and present a patently false portrayal of reality. They are the last remaining remnant of the League of Right Rightness, which we vanquished in 1986 (see timeline). A few independent superheroes remain, and do continue to pester/beat up/ arrest supervillains worldwide, but their strength and numbers are greatly exaggerated by the culture at large.
- One guy's got all the answers (me again).

Testimonials

To show you just how important the work we do is, I rounded up some recent ISS customers (victims) to ask about their experiences with our evil organization. Here's what they had to say:

"He turned my entire family into statues!" – Hans Francis, Pebble Beach, talking about his day with Evil Rodin

"I mith the tathte of brueberrith." – Alith Weith, Rochethter, after being visited by The Tongue Collector

"I wish it had been The Tongue Collector." – Pete Johnson, Lower Columbia, following his encounter with The Junk Shrinker

"Ah-ha. Ahahahaha! AHAHAHAHAHAHA!" – No name given, Gotham City, found mysteriously on a fishing boat

"I'll tell you this much: When they label something as a death ray, they really mean the death part." – Ron T. Foot, Miami, upon his resurrection at the last universe reboot

"I wish they'd stop rebooting the universe just because they decided to go to a casino and they weren't getting sevens." – Maxine Fukimoto, Boston, historian

"Year crazy one been has this." – Official statement from the nation of Papua New Guinea, on the last day of the year in which time there progressed backwards

"Thou must help me! I ain't had a good supper in weeks! Deus non succurro mihi iam. Send mad help, yooooooooo!" – Alex Boccaccio, Florence, lost in time

"She made a monkey out of me." – Popo, formerly Henrietta McDougal, turned into a talking Bonobo chimpanzee by a stray raygun blast when Grrlrilla attempted to turn every band at the Warped Tour into her primate lovers

"Owwwwwwwwwwwwwwwwwwwwwwwww." – Luis Trevizo, Chattanooga, while being shot with PrankTank's Purple Nurple Cannon

The Bottom Line

Hopefully, these figures and testimonials have convinced you that the International Society of Supervillians is the top villainy organization in the world. For the one reader out there who the Psychomonitor is telling me is still doubtful about our legitimacy, enjoy this gift from PrankTank's new Purple Nurple Satellite.

Chapter 1

Motivation*

Meet Max Badguy. He's decided to live up to his full potential and become a supervillain! (His parents, Herb and Candice Badguy, are in real estate.)

---

*   Chapter 1 is sponsored by CRISPY CREAM, "Your teleportation destination since 1938."

Let's make one thing clear right out of the gate:

Revenge isn't enough.

You quite possibly bought this book (or, if you really wanted to get a head start on things, you stole it, and then burned down the bookstore) because you were mad at somebody and wanted to exact some sweet, cold retribution on him or her. Now that's perfectly fine, as anger is a great place to start. But you can hate your boss at Orange Julius all you want, have all the daddy issues in the world, or really want to kill your husband because his breath stinks, and not be anywhere near supervillain material. It might make you a perfect case for the American psycho-pharmaceutical industry (which we supervillains run, naturally), not cathartic therapy sessions in which you threaten children while wearing a domino mask and purple and green jumpsuit while flying around on some mysteriously propelled levitation device.

Hell, somebody may have just up and shot your parents one night while you looked on. That would probably drive someone to some crazy lengths. But honestly, those circumstances would probably make you way more likely to be headed for herodom, and specifically Batmandom, than on the verge of planning out a convoluted plot to poison the city's water supply.

Or let's say you're one of those people who, for no real reason other than your violent urges, bursts into a 7-Eleven, shooting wildly, kidnaps a baby, or robs a card game.

Professional tip: Never rob a supervillain card game. We will kill you, appropriately, with the cards themselves, and then continue playing on your corpse, even though the cards will be all bloody and gross, just to prove a point.

Are you a criminal if you do those things? Oh, you bet you are. Perhaps you're even a terrorist.

Further Pro-tip: Don't confuse terrorists and supervillains. That's slander, pal.

Are you a supervillain? Not even a little bit. You're a standard-issue thug. Deal with it.

SUPERVILLAIN HISTORY FACT:

Many Americans know George Washington as the father of our country, but few are aware that the first U.S. president was actually an early version of what would, in the 20th century, be considered, a supervillain. General Washington's membership in the Freemasons and his wooden teeth, which gained him the nickname Splinterchomp, made him widely known as a "nefaryist," which was a sub-sect of people known for having deformities and being parts of shady, world-conquering organizations. Also, he once viciously murdered a mutated do-gooder who could shape shift into various kinds of fruit trees. That story is often told erroneously.

Beyond simple vengeance and/or psychosis, supervillains need an extra something, an extra drive to do those things that the general populace, or even general criminals, just won't do. You need to go to extreme lengths.

You know who understood that concept pretty damn well? Shakespeare.

No, seriously, check it out:

Hamlet was a guy whose dad got killed by his uncle. So what did he do? He barreled right back to his home country of Denmark and killed the ever-living shit out of his father's killer and whomever else he thought might have had anything to do with the murder. That's some ugly, vengeful stuff right there. But in Shakespeare's world, Hamlet, a cold-blooded killer, is the hero.

In *The Merchant of Venice*, the main character, Antonio, goes out of his way to screw up the life of Shylock, for no other reason than that he is Jewish. Not to boil a classic five-act play down to a sentence or anything, but he essentially makes it so that Shylock either has to give up everything he owns or convert to Christianity. He also spits on Shylock early on in the play, just for kicks. That's some pretty evil stuff, but it falls shy of supervillainy. Antonio's basically a dick, or maybe just a plain old villain.

Macbeth, on the other hand, is a different story. He isn't totally motivated by jealousy, and he isn't just a dick . . . that dude wants to be king. So what does he do? He murders the current king; then he tries to kill a bunch of other guys in jerkins, too. He does it all for power (and because he's pretty crazy). He is a supervillain. (As for lady Macbeth, bitch is also crazy. She's a supervillain, too.)

Now don't get me wrong, just because you want to rule your country and speak in highfalutin language (that is still mostly thinly veiled sexual innuendo), doesn't necessarily make you a prime candidate for the supervillain arts, either. It might conceivably make you a budding politician (evil, yes; supervillainous, no). Neither does outright murderous rage, avarice, a violently skewed sense of justice, or for that matter, plain old insanity. Not even the old-fashioned need to simply prove you're better and smarter than everyone else is a ticket into villainhood.

All those things do help, of course, as sanity is simply just another roadblock to global domination. And without the desire to murder, well, it ain't villainy without murder (or at least the threat of murder). That goes for greed as well. And, come on, every supervillain eventually wants to prove that he or she is the best in the world at everything. Hell, it's in our blood. That's why it's so difficult to get us in a room together without the cleaning crew having to tidy up henchman guts the next morning (more on them in Chapter 7). If I could be frank for a moment, showing up others is a pretty key reason why supervillains generally pick the track of evil instead of the way of red-and-blue tights, cheesy romance, and thinly veiled homoeroticism known as super-herodom. Those guys work together far too well, and they're all humble and shit.

No thank you.

PROFILES IN LAME SUPERVILLAINY

The Spot

History: Dr. Jonathan Ohnn was a C-list scientist working for an A-list supervillain, The Kingpin, trying to figure out how the powers of a B-list superhero, Cloak, worked. After some generic sciency mumbo-jumbo happened, he got sent to another dimension and emerged looking like a Dalmatian.

M.O.: Can teleport using the black, circular portals all over his body. But instead of using them to transport into banks and steal money or to blackmail The Kingpin and take over his empire by learning all his business secrets, he instead decides to use his immense power to simply go directly to Spider-Man so he can lose to him in a fight. Brilliant.

When it comes to having a murderously skewed sense of justice . . . well, that's definitely good (bad) to have in your hip pocket. It's a hell of a justification for doing stuff that just plain makes no sense. For example: If a superhero saves a busload of children from going over a cliff, he or she is clearly an impediment to the natural way of things. Or at least, that's what you keep spouting to yourself as you continue to fight against a guy saving dozens of children. Nature intended for those children in that bus to go over that cliff, you mutter. The hero is hampering the natural order of things. This so called "hero" is anti-nature. He or she must, then, be stopped. *

Really, it takes a combination of some or all of these things to make you a grade-A supervillain in the making. You need the perfect storm of power, madness, bloodlust, jealousy, and, most importantly, a flair for the dramatic.

It's not enough to want to humiliate your old college lab partner for embarrassing you in front of some girl you wanted to get down with; you have to want to do it in a mask and cape. You need more than a mere desire to seize and control a continent with an iron fist; you have to want to do it using an army of robots that look exactly like you. And murder, as necessary as it is, will not get you over that line between plain old crime and glorious super-crime, dear readers. There needs to be an urge in your heart to want to skeletonize people with a heat ray so big that you've got to shoot it from space.

---

* Or maybe you love insects more than people, so you start hassling entomologists (supervillain name idea: Mister Murder Moth) or anyone who ever kills a bug. That could work.

Or getting a radioactive shark to eat some hyperactive vigilante who thinks he should help people by getting all up in your business.

Or using bright-green gas to turn people's lungs inside out.

And during all of that, you have to be compelled to monologue. Constantly.

It's called showmanship, and it's pretty damn well mandatory.

Macbeth had it; talking to a knife floating in front of you before you stab the king to death? Oh yeah, that's some supervillain mojo right there. Of course, Macbeth felt some guilt about what he did, and that's a pretty big problem. We'll be addressing that issue in Chapter 10.

Ultimately, this is what it all boils down to, folks: Murder, rob, plot, and give them a spectacle. In supervillainy, you're not just a genocidal maniac who wipes out entire cities, far from it! What you actually are is a genocidal maniac who gives people the show of their lives before you turn them into thick, purple goo.

Training Exercise 1: Testing Your Mettle

It's one thing to say you have the fire in your belly needed to take on the harsh realities of being an international supervillain, but to actually go out there and do it, and enjoy it, well that's a whole different proposition. So here's an eight-step plan to test your belly-fire quotient.

Step One: Acquire several unnaturally large monkeys.

> This should be relatively easy. Giant monkeys are readily available on most remote jungle islands and at zoos located next to volatile nuclear power facilities.

Step Two: Sic said monkeys on a major American city.

> And we mean major. A giant-monkey rampage in Missoula, Montana, or Winston-Salem, North Carolina, is barely even national news.

Step Three: While the monkeys create chaos, sneak into City Hall.

> All the city's police and emergency personnel, and if they know what's good for them, political leaders will be off dealing with the monkeys. Or they might be dead. Either way, it'll free up the building for you.

Step Four: Steal the city charter.

> It will be in one of two places: Under glass as soon as you walk into City Hall, or in a safe behind a painting in the mayor's office. There are no other options. Be careful, because it

will be on parchment, even if it was rewritten all of fifteen years ago.

Step Five: Replace the charter with a forgery proclaiming that the city is now its own sovereign state, and that you are its supreme leader.

No one will be the wiser.

Step Six: When the mayor absent-mindedly walks in and sees what you're doing (because a superhero stopped your monkey distraction, the bastard), abscond with him.

It helps if you have some kind of flying platform with which you can escape out the window as police and security fire at you.

Step Seven: Threaten to kill the mayor when a meddling superhero confronts you as you're trying to escape to your hidden lair.

It's best to plot your route so that you'll pass over as many bridges and/or imposing skyscrapers as possible.

Step Eight: Escape, preferably after roughing up the hero or embarrassing the mayor.

Releasing another round of giant monkeys would really serve as a great distraction as you rush off and lick your wounds. They're always a great distraction.

If you can do all these things without one qualm of conscience, without feeling like an idiot or ever questioning whether what you're doing is the most efficient way of securing control of the city, then keep reading, friend and fiend.

Chapter 2

Qualifications[*]

Kirby University is the number-one school for dramatic hand gestures.

It's great that you're so amply motivated to destroy all your enemies and proclaim victory from the top of an island shaped like your head; it's good to start somewhere, and those are certainly worthwhile goals (more of which we'll discuss in the next chapter). But before we get there, I must give fair warning: Without the right talents and necessary skills, you still may not make it into the hallowed halls of professional super-evil.

It sounds harsh, I know, but here's some hot truth for you:

Not everybody's cut out to be a supervillain.

Some people, the average rabble out there; well, they deserve to be trampled, either as helpless civilians, expendable henchmen, or hapless, overhyped "heroes."

That difficult standard is true in any profession, of course. Some people want to be professional writers, for instance, of novels and screenplays and great works of high art and import. But most end up writing silly little fake how-to guides about how to become a supervillain. They are sad, depressing people, these wannabe writers. They need emotional help, because they know they will, probably very soon, die alone and penniless, with nothing of value to their name. That's just how the world works.

But I digress.

You're going to need some credentials if you want to be respected in professional villain circles. There are plenty of guys out there, total amateurs, running around with no direction, no know-how, and no respect. We snicker at these guys behind their backs and stick lit matches in their butt cracks at supervillain expo events. Don't be one of these guys.

Here's how to avoid the old flame-ass:

Education

Like it or not, if you're interested in the villain game, you're going to want some degrees, and I'm not talking community college degrees, I'm talking Graduate degrees.

It would take me about a thousand hours to list for you all the supervillains whose names are preceded by "doctor," "professor," or at least, "nurse." There's some inexplicable force in higher education that drives people to villainy, and vice-versa. Maybe it's the constant pressure of getting papers, theses, and what have you done on time or the persistent badgering from professors or dealing with smug fraternity assholes in Birkenstocks and pink polo shirts all day.

Or, more likely, it has something to do with the fact that college campuses are places where curious students and disgruntled instructors can perform the ancient and mysterious art known as mad science. There's test tubes and beakers and shit everywhere, which means there's all kinds of opportunities for making poisonous gas bombs or building clone robots of yourself or developing chemicals that will transform innocent, wholesome, and delicious milk into a potion that turns everyone who drinks it into lizard-man hybrids that you can summon to come break you out of prison. (Trust me on that one.)

There's also something about professordom that just kicks people into villainy mode as well. I'll attribute that to the fact that grading papers all night would make pretty much anybody want to murder an entire city's worth of people. Or, it's possibly the small contingent of college students who have a near-unflappable tendency to regularly become superheroes. Stupid young bastards with their bright eyes and minds full of hope. We will crush them! Grrrrrrrrraaaaagggggghhh!

Moving on, I would be remiss if I didn't mention that not all supervillains have to live in some ivory tower. Many are also medical doctors, dentists, psychologists, attorneys, and, of course, businesspeople.

Yes indeed, the MBA can be a supervillain degree, too, so long as you can become the founder/chairman/CEO/president of your own company, the resources of which you can use to hunt down and destroy your over-powered nemesis. The cool thing about it is that, no matter how many times you get arrested or outed as an international super-criminal, your business conglomerate will always continue to exist somehow, and you'll always be the boss.

I know that statement's in no way based in any sort of objective reality, but you can't argue with the way of things, which are laid out in several decades' worth of comics. People with long, long rap sheets always manage to come back to respectability, just like superheroes who are maligned when

SUPERVILLAIN HISTORY FACT:

Though quite evil, Adolf Hitler, Pol Pot, Joseph Stalin, and Fidel Castro were not, at any point in their lifetimes, supervillains. They were never part of a supervillain group and never created a supervillain name for themselves. The only super-villain who was also a 20th century dictator was Benito Mussolini, whose widely-known moniker, Il Duce, was Italian for "Commander Crossword." The clues he left for heroes at the scenes of his various crimes were structured in the same way as crossword clues. His catchphrase was, "What's a five-letter word for DEATH?"

some impersonator starts robbing banks in their costumes and immediately get exonerated the second someone realizes that just about anybody could sew together some blue spandex. Look, we don't write the rules; that's just the way it works in the world of superheroes and supervillains. Live with it, 'cause it ain't changing; not if we have anything to say about it.

Breeding

"But King Oblivion," I hear through my trusty Psychomonitor, "what am I, a lowly high school dropout and generally blithering idiot, to do? I don't have the time or the money to get a GED, and, frankly, I would fail out of college, because I am intellectually inferior to you in every way."

Thank you for your honesty, reader. (Though you should note that I prefer to be addressed as "sire.") The very fact that you're even struggling through reading this book is a testament to your commitment to the evil arts (unless you forced someone to read it to you, in which case, that's the kind of initiative that can get you places).

Luckily, you have a few options . . . like stealing a diploma. But you could also accept that not all villains need to be super-brilliant masterminds like me. Some can simply be thuggish brutes, which we brainy villains like to call "the muscle."

We'll get more into those distinctions later on in Chapter 4, but for now, rest assured that there is supervillainy without higher education, albeit a form that has more to do with punching and bank robbing than death rays and world domination.

So set your sights low, non-doctor-and-professor set. That is, unless you have the great luck to have been born a member of some country's royal family or hold the title of some other type of nobleman or woman. Then, you can order anybody you want around without ever having to learn anything of any kind. So be warned, if you're not a duke or a lordess or something, and you have no mental aptitude whatsoever, you may want to consider going back in time and setting it up so that your ancestors offed a baron or something. Just putting that out there.

Experience

Now, before you go out there and try to turn Australia upside-down, Ph.D.s and duchesses, you need to know that it's going to take more than a fancy degree or some kick-ass title to make your name in this business.

Just like anything else in this world, you've got to get out there and work your way up the ladder. But how do you do that? Well, there's a few ways that you can put your stamp on this art we call supervillainin'.

Franchising

Show some entrepreneurial spirit and start your own operation. Acquire some capital (aka: Kill and then assume the identity of a bigwig capitalist), and then brand and make yourself known locally. After that, expand to a regional operation. Eventually, if your work is bad enough, people will notice, and you'll be a national or even global outfit.

Henching

Just like the old-fart corporate CEO who always likes to tell the story about how he started out in the mailroom (or for today's "young professional," a lowly intern), you can reach the heights of supervillainy by getting work as a lowly henchman. Stay loyal, do the work, and maybe, one day, you'll take the reins when your boss-villain retires or kicks the bucket. (aka: Kill your boss and assume his or her identity.)

Petty Crime

Rob some banks, beat up some superheroes, maybe set off a bomb or two. Your objective is to get on the news. Catch the eye of some bigger-name supervillains in your area. Make your services available to them whenever they need to kidnap the governor's daughter and don't want to get their hands dirty. Soon, you'll be in their inner circle and right where you want to be. (Or, you could find someone in their inner circle, kill him or her, and assume his or her identity.)

The Superhero Switcheroo

One very quick way into big-time supervillainy is to become known as a superhero before taking some sort of dramatic turn to the dark side. This kind of thing happens pretty often (we have a way better dental plan and our outfits are simply much more comfortable), and usually with pretty good (that is, bad) results. Nothing gets the smelly, hero-loving masses more riled up than a heel turn. (If you're uncertain about how to become a superhero, well, this ain't the right book for you, hoss. Maybe you could kill one and steal his or her identity.)

Nepotism

Be the son, daughter, nephew, cousin, brother, sister, or in-law of a successful supervillain, and affix yourself right onto his or her evil teat. (If you don't have any supervillain family members, then kill the family member of a supervillain and assume his or her identity.)

Kill someone close to a villain and assume his or her identity

This is fairly standard practice.

With enough work, you'll eventually work your way up to a fairly high position in the world of pro evil. But, and I should make this as clear as I can, don't shoot for my seat. If you even try to sit in my chair made of skulls perched atop a solid fire column deep within our subterranean fortress, I will personally incinerate you, and it won't be instantaneous. It'll take days—painful, painful days.

Let's move on.

Ten Celebrities We'd Like to Recruit

One thing we in the supervillain world are always looking to create is a higher profile. In today's world, what better way to do that than by recruiting some famous celebrities? Here are our top-ten choices, the people we feel will bring us the most attention, but whom we also feel have got what it takes for this supervillain life.

1. Tom Cruise

Qualifications: A certain religious group he's in big with. He's an Operating Thetan level VII, which means he's probably in direct contact with the Overlord Xenu himself. And yes, the story goes that Scientologists hate Xenu and stuff, because he trapped the Thetans in their meat bodies. But if we can use Cruise to get to the overlord, even under the pretense of an attack, we'll take it, just to get Xenu on the team.

Liabilities: He believes in some crazy shit, like the existence of Overlord Xenu.

Bottom line: Tom Cruise is crazy, y'all. But he may be able to get us in touch with an evil galactic overlord. And even if he can't, well then hell, we'll take the chance to crib some notes from the people in charge of the church of Scientology, who seem to have a pretty good (bad) evil system worked out.

2. Katy Perry

Qualifications: Clearly, she is a master of hypnotism.

Liabilities: We'll have to work really hard to not become mesmerized by her off-putting, yet somehow insanely catchy, mind-controlling songs, all of which are brilliantly named after older, also very-popular songs.

Bottom line: Obnoxious? Certainly. But we'll deal with it for the collective consciousness of the masses.

3. Stephen Colbert

Qualifications: Well, for one, he owns Captain America's shield, and we'd really like to get our hands on that puppy. Also, he has the power to name and define all the major threats facing America and the world. If we get him, then we can finally overtake bears and zombies as the biggest threats around (we've been gunning for that spot for years). Plus, he seems to have some sort of teleportation device that allows him to go into the offices of members of Congress so that he can ridicule them. Double-plus, we're really itching to get that Colbert bump.

Liabilities: With that Super PAC of his, it may be hard to get his attention. It's tough for even us to compete with those corporate political bucks.

Bottom line: We must have him, and his Threat Down.

4. Sarah Palin

Qualifications: She unsuccessfully ran for vice president, gave up her job as Alaska governor mid-term, had a failed reality show about her family, and people still think she's got what it takes to be president. Her qualifications are that she somehow gets people to think she has qualifications despite her lack of qualifications. That's the most incredible power of deception we've ever seen.

Liabilities: Her accent is perhaps too powerful a weapon for even us. Also, we'd prefer to avoid having her blabbermouth grandbaby-daddy chattering about us all on ET or whatever.

Bottom line: Sometimes you just need a good old American hockey mom to go out there and work up crowds to maim some superheroes for ya now, dontcha know.

5. Justin Bieber

Qualifications: He commands a massive army of tween and teenage girls, all of whom follow his every move. If we could get our hands on him, then we would be in control of a wave of text messages, tweets and incoherent conversations unlike the world has ever seen. Imagine it: Millions of evil denizens with *Twilight* backpacks and hot pink cell phones. It would be a thing of beauty.

Liabilities: You can only hear the word "baby" so many times before you start setting things on fire.

Bottom line: Once we obtain the loyalty of his followers, he is no longer necessary. We'll get rid of him, and then get our colleague Chameleo to wear his face or something.

6. Sarah Silverman

Qualifications: Anyone who's ever read a profile of Sarah Silverman in just about any magazine will remember reading the part where the writer states, as if it's never been said before, that she can get away with saying things most comedians can't because she's a pretty, mousy-voiced woman. And yeah, it's been said a billion times, but it's true. Which makes us think that she might be able to *do* anything and get away with it, too. Like, I dunno, perhaps sink Japan.

Liabilities: She'd probably spend a lot of time going on and on about how marrying her dog is hilarious or some other dumb shit like that.

Bottom line: We'll take some crappy jokes if it means we'll be insulated from all world law-enforcement agencies and military organizations.

7. Morgan Freeman

Qualifications: The amazing power of narration. Whatever Morgan Freeman says, happens. So we'd really like to arrange it so that wherever we go, he's a few yards above us in a helicopter with a bullhorn, saying that we just escaped or stole all the money or vaporized The Flash.

Liabilities: Could you believe this guy as a villain? No, you could not. You saw *Wanted*, right? See what I mean?

Bottom line: We don't need him to be evil, we only need him to say evil things, so that they'll come true.

8. Lady Gaga

Qualifications: She's already got the look down, and at times she scares even us. Plus, as you may have surmised, supervillains love to play poker.

Liabilities: The dramatic reveal of her villain name may sound more to the unfamiliar like baby talk than evil grandstanding.

Bottom line: A villain who wears nothing but meat would be both novel and delicious during after parties.

9. Will Smith

Qualifications: None, really (except for perhaps an intricate knowledge of how much parents just don't understand). No, recruiting Will Smith would be a symbol, that even the nicest guy in Hollywood, the perennial hero, can be corrupted. I mean, even when the guy plays a jerk, he still ends up looking like a good guy. We need to fix that.

Liabilities: The theme to "The Fresh Prince of Bel-Air" and the song "Summertime" are impossible to get out of your head, and if Smith was around, they'd be in there *all the time*.

Bottom line: If we are to prove that all that is good can be made evil, we need Will Smith.

10. Oprah

Qualifications: She is Oprah.
Liabilities: She is Oprah.
Bottom line: *She is Oprah.*

Health

Believe it or not, life is not necessarily a prerequisite for becoming a supervillain. Sure, most supervillains are among the living, and in a lot of ways, being alive does make things easier (even when it's your own dead body, the smell of rotting flesh is just plain overpowering). But death isn't a total impediment to super-crime. We've worked with zombies, ghosts, demons, wraiths, banshees, spirits, vampires, Frankenstein monsters, mummies, and other undead and/or immortal beings before, and for the most part, they do pretty well (badly) for themselves. Sometimes their jaw falls off during monologues and stuff, but hey, we all have our problems.

To a less extreme extent, major infirmities, such as being confined to a wheelchair, having a terminal disease or out-and-out being really ugly are actually big benefits when it comes to villainy. The more decrepit and disgusting you are, the better (worse), we say.

PROFILES IN LAME SUPERVILLAINY

Ten-Eyed Man

History: Philip Reardon, a Vietnam vet, who was partially blinded when he got hit with some grenade shrapnel, was fully blinded one night after a fight with Batman led to an explosion that burned his retinas. Afterward, a scientist somehow re-attached his optic nerves to the tips of his fingers.

M.O.: The shrapnel must have also damaged Mr. Reardon's brain, because he thinks it is a good idea to go after Batman, who he blames for blinding him, under the moniker Ten-Eyed Man while wearing a costume calling attention to the fact that he can only see through his fingers. As a result, Batman, being the world's greatest detective, deduces that he can simply throw something at the Ten-Eyed Man, shout "Catch!," blind the guy, and win.

Age

As we mentioned earlier, heroes always tend to be young, plucky types with great hair. In supervillainy, we are much less discriminating when it comes to the age groups we'll accept into our malevolent hordes. But a few age groups seem to really dominate our business:

- The very old
- The very young (evil children are creepy as hell, and we like that)
- Middle-aged men
- Super-sexy hot babes in their twenties and thirties (our favorite category)
- Immortals

If you don't fit into any of these groups, then you may still have a future in villainy; but be warned: If you're some hotshot high-school student or college kid coming in here with your barrel chest and well-defined chin, chances are we will shoot first and ask questions later. Ugly yourself up, fella.

Have You Got What It Takes for Treachery? The Supervillain Qualifications Quiz

If you're still not sure whether you fit the supervillain mold, ask yourself the following questions:

1. Have you recently been, or plan to be, permanently disfigured as the result of a fall into a vat of acid?

2. Are you the monarch of one or more fictional Eastern European countries?

3. Have you ever killed your own parents? Have you done it often?

4. Have you ever been a part of a grand scientific experiment gone awry?
   a. Did it involve radiation? Metal tentacles? Gigantism?

5. If so, were you turned into some sort of half-man, half-animal hybrid, or a person whose body consists of some common material, such as water, rock, or spiders?

6. When you speak, do you hiss?

7. Is one of your limbs made out of something other than flesh and bone, such as metal, a very large salmon, or a tiny little person?

8. Have you ever created a clone of yourself or someone else?

9. Are you a spandex-wearing cat burglar who also enjoys being a huge cock tease?

10. When you're giving a speech, would someone transcribing it be compelled to do so in ALL CAPITAL LETTERS?

11. When committing a crime or doing some other covert activity, is your first instinct to leave unnecessary clues behind?

12. Is your ideal home an island that is named after you?

13. Do people rarely or never see your face, either because it is often obscured by a mask or people just always happen to be viewing you from behind?

14. Do you often announce what you are doing at any given time, even if no one else is around?

15. Have you survived being a passenger on an exploding helicopter, airplane, or blimp?

16. Cloaks: Yes or no?

17. Do you often use the word "insolence" in day-to-day conversation?

18. If some guy started flying around in the city where you live, saving runaway subway trains and stopping attempted burglaries in alley-ways, would your first instinct be to strap him to a gurney and shoot lasers at him?

19. Are you bald?
    a. Are there nodes implanted into your scalp?

20. Are you an immortal cosmic being who eats planets to survive?

If you answered "yes" to more than seven of these questions, you are well on your way to supervillainy. If you answered more than fifteen in the affirmative, you can join the ISS right now. If you answered number twenty with a "yes," then thanks for reading, Galactus.

Chapter 3

Goals*

Combining goals can lead to unusual and counterproductive behavior.

---

* Chapter 3 is sponsored by The OH SHIT I AM A SURPRISE GIANT catalog, "Casual business and formal clothing for the big and tall and huge and enormous gentleman."

About one hundred years ago, the man who is now generally regarded as the first true supervillain, Heinrich Misanthroach, otherwise known as Dr. Blattarius (a name he took from the Latin word for "cockroach," because he was half roach), said, "In all things, my treacherous sons, hatred . . . always, hatred. But know this: Your hatred must be focused. You must know your limits. More importantly, you must know your desires, and work night and day to acquire them. Narrow your misanthropy, develop your plan, and execute."

"Personally, I want to kill that asshole Mr. Wonderful."

And so he did. That is, until Mr. Wonderful came back to life (superheroes have a terrible habit of doing that) and destroyed Dr. Blattarius' device designed to re-write all telegrams with messages demanding humanity's unyielding obedience to him. Mr. Wonderful unfairly dogged him with a flurry of punches when Doc B's back was turned (that's the only way superheroes ever do anything). But we all heard that story in evil grade school.

I bring up that old saw to make this point, which is one of the many things Dr. Blattarius taught us: You have to know what you want, and you can't spread yourself too thin. It is imperative that you figure out what the one thing you most desire is, and you must make sure to work toward that one thing. Nothing else. World domination is a fine goal, but if you're simultaneously working on humiliating your greatest enemy, while avenging the death of a relative and making yourself rich, it just ain't in the cards. Plus, we at the ISS already kind of have the whole world domination thing all wrapped up, and you don't want to go stepping on our toes. So here's a few of the other common goals for your garden-variety rookie supervillain. Choose the one that fits you best.

SUPERVILLAIN HISTORY FACT

Olympic gold-medalist sprinter Jesse Owens spent quite a few successful years holding up banks as the supervillain Dash Demon. His career was cut short, sadly, when he let his hubris get the best of him and he was apprehended while attempting to rob a 201-meter-long bank.

Revenge

Just now, my Psychomonitor almost exploded from all the readers out there wondering, "But didn't you say earlier that revenge wasn't enough of a motivator for aspiring super-villains?" And yes, I did say that. But you may have also noticed further down in that chapter where I said that the most important motivator for villainy is *theatricality*. (And if you turn my words against me again, I swear I will cut off your hands and feet and reattach them backwards.) Revenge is a great goal for supervillains, but it's a requirement that you achieve it in the grandest way possible.

To make sure we're perfectly clear, if your idea of exacting revenge on someone is to key his or her car, then you're not a supervillain. If you choose to get him or her back by crushing their car or the building where he or she works with a twenty-ton key, then you're well on your way.

But make no mistake about it, supervillainous revenge usually doesn't come easily. It has to be more of a lifetime endeavor. You must completely hate the subject of your torment with so much of your being that it consumes you. A key phrase here is "biding your time." To put it another way, here's a question that may give you an idea of whether or not revenge is going to be your number one objective: Would you be willing to devote years of your life to leaving the country, permanently affixing a mask to your face or otherwise obscuring your identity, training your body to make it a living weapon, harping incessantly on the person who wronged you, and plotting for your eventual return and retribution?

Basically, could you be the Count of Monte Cristo? Not the literal Count, though that might help too, but the character from the book of the same name. To have been the protagonist of a book, that guy was a bona fide bad-ass supervillain. So look to Alexandre Dumas for your guide, avenging villains.

The only place where Edmond Dantes is not necessarily the best guidepost for your future as a revenge-based super-villain is in his grounds for revenge. That guy had a lot of good reasons for going back and killing the shit out of his enemies. He was accused of being a traitor, got condemned because some cat wanted to save his political career, and later found out that his rival married his fiancée. That's some hardcore wronging, and those guys probably deserved what was coming to them.

For your purposes, you can take out all your rage on the first person who stops one of your early criminal exploits, someone who makes you look foolish (preferably when you were in grade school), or a dude who accidentally scuffs your sneakers on the bus. Frankly, the more ridiculous your reasoning for hating the object of your bitterness, the better (worse).

PROFILES IN LAME SUPERVILLAINY

Magpie

History: Some lady with no discernible powers decided it would be a good idea to commit crimes while drawing no attention to herself what-soever by dressing as a character from *The Rocky Horror Picture Show*. Then she went and named herself Magpie, after the incredibly threatening, tiny little bird.

M.O.: Keeping up with the bird theme, Magpie steals jewels and other valuable items named for birds, and replaces those items with decoy booby traps. Get it? Booby? Like the bird? That's how Magpie rolls. Also, she chooses to fight Batman and Superman with a handgun and a length of chain.

Riches

Movies and comic books are the scourges of our villainous existence, even more so than those sulking, holier-than-thou superheroes (see Chapter 10), they tend to portray us villains as people who steal money as only a means to an end. We need it for our sick kids, to carry out our mad experiments, or we just like to burn it up because we're so anarchic, or so those bastard, non-villainous writers assume.

And yeah, we know some guys like that, sure. But don't get it twisted. In large part, we love money, and find that wealth can often be a worthwhile goal in and of itself. The more of it we can get our hands on, the happier we are; partially because it allows us to buy up more resources for our death rays and torture chambers and to pay off our henchmen and/or bookies (when we choose to pay them, rather than just turning them into platypi), but also because, hey, we like to live well too.

Giant thrones made out of skulls don't come cheap, folks. Plus, if you've looked on Craigslist lately, cavernous yet mansion-like underground and/or undersea lairs are vastly expensive, even if you steal all the materials needed to build them. So unless you want to locate your base of operations at the Home Depot, where you'll also stock shelves, you may want to look into robbing some banks (perhaps with a magnet that allows you to steal banks in their entirety) or becoming a serious super jewel thief.

You know what else? Diving into a giant pile of money is a great feeling, too. Trust me on this one. You're going to want to figure out a way to do that once or twice a day if you even have the slightest hint of money lust in your cold, black heart.

Justice

We went over this fairly thoroughly in Chapter 1, but to hammer home the point, if you see some kind of problem with a guy going around stopping airplanes from crashing, you should go deal with that, whether society understands it or not.

Just because a bunch of big-headed idiots in suits decided to write a bunch of shit down and call them "laws," doesn't mean that's what's right. Show them what's right, pilgrim. Show them with your bare hands. Even if that means razing their capitol building right off the ground while reciting lines from *The Art of War*.

Violence for Its Own Sake

Think hard about this scenario: A crowd of hundreds gathers in an auditorium to watch the latest performance of the great magician, Classico the Magnificent. Ah, but the performer tonight is not Classico at all. It's you, tuxedoed and mustachioed; the perfect double for Classico as he takes a quick, unconscious (and nude) break in the dumpster behind the performance hall. You take the stage, performing admirably enough that the audience simply thinks Classico is on the bottle again. Finally, you reach the night's final, show-stopping illusion, which involves sawing your assistant in half. But surprise! Your assistant is not Classico's assistant at all. It's the famous superheroine, Infinity Woman, who you captured earlier in the day with your army of tiny robot men. You bring her out, the crowd recognizes her, and you remove your disguise, revealing yourself to be a supervillain extraordinaire. Then, the coup de grâce: You unveil the giant, diamond-tipped buzz saw with which you have replaced the trick saw. As the frightened crowd looks on, cowers, or attempts to escape, they'll only find out that the doors are welded shut, as you begin to lower the saw, laughing heartily.

Would you describe your reaction to that scenario as being horrified? Shocked? Sickened? Well, that's understandable. But if you don't feel any of those things, if you feel your hair standing on end with excitement, your blood pressure rising, a demented smile creeping up on your face and a little bit of pee hitting your underwear as you read ever more details of Infinity Woman's demise, then you're just the type of sociopath who may be well into violence for violence's sake. (Just keep it to yourself, OK? You kind of gross the rest of us out.)

For some villains, the ends of villainy really aren't that complicated. There is one thing we love to see, and we love to see it as often as we can: the suffering of others. But we want more than the mere pedestrian carnage of blowing up an abortion clinic or tearing through a civic center with an uzi. That's far too simplistic, and, frankly, quite uncivilized.

We need gigantic, Rube Goldberg-style death traps. We need to horrify and traumatize the innocents, and, most passionately, we need to build the anticipation to that sweet, sweet moment when the superhero's head dips ever so gingerly into that giant pool filled with radioactive hammerhead sharks that you've had sitting around for the past several months.

Proving a Point

This goal is pretty similar to revenge, but with a twist. Rather than petty revenge or meaningless violence, you're more interested in pettily proving that you're always right about meaningless stuff. No unnecessary emotion or personal vendettas here.

But it's not that sort of proving-them-right mentality that leads to the classic skewed sense of justice. This one's different, in that it's more about proving how beautifully sane you are, and how incredibly brilliant you've always been, than some kind of pedestrian crazy-man hand-of-God garbage.

Maybe they teased you at school. Or your boss pulled the plug on your ongoing research on how to cure your wife, who is terminally ill with a stab wound to the brain. Or they accidentally turned on the machine that makes people half guinea pig while you were still in there cleaning. Perhaps you are a leader among a special sub sect of human beings with special powers others shun and don't understand. (Thanks for reading, Magneto.) Whatever the case may be, things would have been so much easier, and none of this would have ever happened if they had just listened.

Ah, but with your villainous schemes, you can make them listen. You can chain them to the wall and make them watch as you hold their families captive and play old footage of their mistakes. Or, you could hypnotize them into understanding. Either way, they will become believers.

Sexual Satisfaction

Hey, man, if the only way you can get your rocks off is to put on a cloak, stick your hand out, and monologue for fifteen minutes about dominions and hells on earth, then the priesthood or villainy are pretty much your only choices.

But at least we let you have actual sex, too, if you're into that.

Branding Baseness: Nine Corporations To Emulate

You know who's great at getting people to believe all the shit they tell them while still carrying on heinous deeds? Major multinational corporations, that's who. Even I, the master of all villainy, could learn a thing or two from those guys, especially these nine, who have really taken evil PR to new levels.

McDonald's

What they get right: Think back to when you were four years old. Where did you want to eat all day, every day? That's right. Under those big yellow arches. So many impressionable children have been sucked in to the vortex of McDonald's fat and sodium that it's almost magical. And, as a bonus, creepy clown mascot! (And creepy purple monstrosity mascot and creepy perverted burglar mascot.)

What needs work: It's great public relations, but really, McDonald's did you have to go and start your own huge charity for kids? That ain't evil, man.

Google

What they get right: In addition to creating web applications that invade just about every portion of users' personal lives, from their phone messages to their website ads and stats to their travel, Google has also created the greatest database of private personal interests in history. Every search anyone types into their search engine is recorded and logged somewhere, and forever attached to that user. It's a blackmail goldmine.

What needs work: The company is far too kind to its employees. Gourmet food? On-site recreation? Come on, Google. Much more of that and our henchmen are going to expect to be treated like human beings or something. They even have the motto, "Don't be evil." That's prejudice.

Volkswagen

What they get right: Taking a car basically created by Hitler and making it trendy in the United States for like fifty years? Ballsy.

What needs work: Their unshakable connection to hippie-stink takes away a lot of their evil viability.

Apple

What they get right: They've littered the whole globe with tiny little portable machines designed to pump sound into people's ears and track their movements. Loads of potential there. Also, they're great at childishly assaulting their competition while still seeming to keep the high ground. It's like a bully that quotes Proust while beating other kids up.

What needs work: They've done a great job of setting the groundwork, but it's time to set the plan into action, Apple! Start pumping secret messages of anarchy into peoples' ears already, guys!

Goldman Sachs

What they get right: They bet on the housing industry collapsing in 2008 and profited from it.

What needs work: The only problem? We didn't think of that.

AIG

What they get right: Despite completely mismanaging themselves, greedily grabbing cash hand over fist and showing no concern for their clients, they managed to convince the government to give them billions of dollars. That's the dream, folks.

What needs work: Why only rely on one government? It's time to pick up, move to France, and start the whole thing over, AIG. That racket's just too beautiful not to try again.

RJ Reynolds

What they get right: Continuing to sell cigarettes that are known to cause cancer while trying to excuse it by making half-assed anti-smoking ads? That's slimy with a capital S. And brilliant.

What needs work: Cigarettes are great and all, but why not develop something that kills people more quickly? Like, maybe a little stick that sends thousands of tiny man-eating gorillas down someone's throat?

News Corp

What they get right: The company that owns the Fox networks and several right-wing newspapers manages to constantly criticize our trash culture while simultaneously contributing to it more than just about anyone else. Obviously, this is a plan to confuse the populace into submission.

What needs work: Couldn't you guys get a better spokesman for your world takeover plot than Hannity?

Blizzard
<u>What they get right</u>: World of Warcraft is the finest evil plot ever concocted. It makes people inert, suggestible and unproductive. And it's been doing it, without interruption, for years now.
<u>What needs work</u>: Not a thing.

Power

For some, being in charge is what it's all about, and politics involves too much baby kissing and pretending to care about what the public wants. Supervillainy presents a more direct approach:

1. Build gun that freezes rivers.
2. Alert people that you have such a gun.
3. Assume the throne of power.

Of course, there's the sneakier way of going about it, too:

1. Stage an alien invasion.
2. Swoop in and kill the alien "leader," who is actually one of your own henchmen.
3. Live in a castle.

However you take over, there's a really nice feeling that comes from wearing the crown (I know, I'm a king) and being able to crush just about anybody you want under your big, regal thumb. But remember, if power's your thing, we're going to impose some standards on you.

- Want to take over a city and rule over it with an iron fist? Go for it.
- Cities too small for you? You need a whole U.S. state? Take your pick of any Dakota.
- Countries more your speed?
  You could pretty much walk into any place that ends with "-stan," and they'd probably ask you to be in charge.

But if global domination is your thing—and I can't stress this enough—it's our thing, too . . . and we've got way more genetically altered mutant monster men on staff than you can even imagine.

Mischief

I've been going on and on about greed and violence and grasping your hatred—harming the body and the wallet—but that doesn't always have to be your goal. If you want to simply drive some unsuspecting soul mad through soul-crushing psychological torment, have at it. But it's tough. It takes a light touch. The best example of that technique is the story of an oddly-named villain who dedicated himself to creating mayhem for one of the ancestors of the guy who would eventually become the hero Super-Slug. It's been passed down through the villain generations, and we share it with you here.

Mr. Fairweather Butterscotch sat in his study, preparing for a relaxing evening of sitting quietly and speaking to no one, when he heard a violent crash outside his window.

Mortified, Mr. Butterscotch slid into his robe and stumbled out into the garden, a lit candle his only light source in the nearly impenetrable darkness. He called out into the night, morbidly curious as to the motivations of this sudden visitor.

"Hello?" he asked to no one in particular. "Is someone there?"

Mr. Butterscotch scoured the grounds, oh so familiar from his childhood days of play and laughter, when this house was his father's and his only cares were those of any other young boy, so very innocent: diabetes, obesity, and peripheral artery disease.

He checked the greenhouse, the stables, the croquet course, and the servants' quarters—emptied for a sure night of lower-class rambunction, and found little more than the usual faunae and florae, maintained so wonderfully by the staff.

As his apprehension and his candlewick began to dwindle, a quietly falling rain began to float languidly from the clouds, aimless and lazy, in no real hurry to meet with the ground below for its evening slumber. Satisfied that his search had all been for naught, and perhaps his imagination had finally taken hold of his mind, Mr. Butterscotch began his deliberate walk back toward the main house.

Mr. Butterscotch dug in his pocket for the main house key, wondering to himself whether he was more prone to spend an evening in quiet contemplation or silent introspection. Before he had a chance to come to his decision, though, he caught the sight of a spectre out of the corner of his eye, moving quickly across the yard.

"Who's there?" he whispered.

As if on cue, a dark figure stepped out into the light. Mr. Butterscotch identified it immediately. He knew this was coming eventually, even though he had prayed that it never would. He swallowed his fear and addressed his assailant.

"Arrhythmia," he gulped. "We finally meet."

The apparition did not respond, motionless and silent, standing prone, as if waiting for the perfect moment to strike.

The standoff continued, the moments passing like decades, until Mr. Butterscotch could no longer stand the torture.

"What do you want, you vile creature?" he asked.

And before he could stop it, before he could move, Arrhythmia had pulled Mr. Butterscotch's underwear over his head, drawn a mustache on his face and scurried right off with his wallet, (with his credit cards and pictures of his dog in there and everything).

"Damn you, Arrhythmia!" Mr. Butterscotch cried into the rainy night sky, his knees crashing into the mud beneath him, the elastic of his tighty whities digging into his forehead. "Damn youuuuu!"

* * *

"Excuse me, waiter?"

"Yes, sir, how may I be of service to you?"

"I don't mean to complain, but I believe there may be an angina pectoris in my soup."

"Oh dear, Mr. Butterscotch, I am so terribly sorry! I'll be having a word with the chef about this!"

"Well, I'm not sure that's necessary . . . "

"Oh, sir, it most certainly is! I'll bring him out here so we can both talk to him! You just wait here!"

"But – wait! I don't –"

"What's all this about my soup having a symptom of myocardial ischemia in it?"

"Um . . . actually, Mr. Chef, I didn't mean to make a stir, I just . . . wait a minute. You look a bit familiar. Do I know you?"

"Perhaps, Mr. Butterscotch, you do! Hahahahahaha! And away I go!"

"What – what is this? Underwear . . . pulled over head! Mustache . . . drawn on face! Wallet . . . gone! I don't . . . Arrhythmia! Oooooh! I'll get you!"

* * *

Heart Murmur Township Police Department, 10/31, 3:32 P.M., Official Report of Events

A middle-aged gentleman in a three-piece suit, claiming to be Mr. Fairweather Butterscotch of 3313 Mitral Valve Prolapse Lane, enters station, asking to speak with someone in charge of heart disease related assaults. He tells the presiding officer, a Sergeant, about a series of pranks/attacks that have been allegedly perpetrated on him over the past several weeks, all of which he reported having resulted in codes 301(a) {wallet theft}, 1201 {vandalism by mustache drawing}, and 19(p-16) {underwear pulled over head}. The sergeant takes down all of Mr. Butterworth's information, assures him that someone would look into the case and files a report. He then performs a 301(a), a 1201, and a 19(p-16) on Mr. Butterscotch. IAD and the attorney general's office are looking into the incident and how Sgt. A. Rhythmia was hired.

* * *

The Journal of the Illustrious Fairweather Butterscotch, Esq.
November 12, Thursday
Dear Journal,

I have done something today of which I am less than proud.

Under great duress from the recent harassment a certain unnamed party has decided to continually and unfeelingly impinge upon me, I took my troubles to a seller of sexual release, or, in more pedestrian terms, a prostitute.

In any other circumstance, it would be anathema for me to procure such services, but with these recent troubles, I have yet to find any other way to ameliorate my considerable stress and trauma. And so, it was with a heavy heart that I called a number I found in the yellow pages that claimed to discreetly send a "companion" to my abode.

She arrived promptly, and I must say she was very becoming and professional. Before any other words were exchanged, she laid down the ground rules for our encounter: no bruising, no intimations of anything beyond business, no going back on what is decided beforehand, etc. I agreed to them.

I asked her name, which she told me was Reynaudse Syndromme – her parents hailed from Paris, and I welcomed her to my home with a glass of my finest '68 Cabernet Sauvignon, which we both enjoyed greatly.

As we sipped the vintage, we began to negotiate the details of what would occur during our encounter. I made several very specific requests, and once we were satisfactorily finished with our beverages, we entered the bedroom to complete our transaction.

She left silently, as I had requested, and I thanked her for her compliance with all my admittedly unusual specifications. As she walked down the drive to her car, she glanced back at me and smiled, playfully holding up the wallet that I had asked she take with her.

I smiled back, my underwear pulled nearly to my eyes, a mustache drawn to such detail on my face that it almost fooled me in the mirror later that evening. It was the first genuine smile I had managed in weeks.

I wonder if I shall see her again.

Training Exercise 2: Knowing Your Desires

You may think you know what you want the end result of your evil exploits to be, but will those goals stay with you once you put your dastardly devisements into practice? Put yourself in the following scenario. Based on how you react, you may want to re-think your ultimate ambitions.

Along with a small group of villainous colleagues, you break through the defenses of the do-gooder stronghold Superhero Tower and enter. Once inside, you . . .

A. . . . head straight for the heroes' conference room, dispatching anyone who gets in your way. You use the cosmic wishing machine you brought with you to clear the room of all the heroes huddled within it. When the room is emptied, you recline in the seat at the head of the conference table and claim the building for your own.

B.   . . . attempt to kill everyone and everything in sight, including the other members of your invasion force.

C.   . . . find the superhero who, years ago, beat you out for the lead in your middle school's production of *Our Town*. Upon coming face-to-face with the object of your life-long hatred, you say, "Now I am the Stage Director, and you, fool, are Farmer McCarthy," before grabbing him and teleporting him to a theater where he is forced to stand onstage while a robot audience shoots lasers at him.

D.   . . . use the power of magi-science, a combination of wizardry and physics you advocated in college and which led to your being laughed out of school, to alter the molecules of the tower's bricks and make the entire building collapse on itself. (It just so happens that Superhero Tower is right next to where you went to college, so everyone there sees it happen.)

E.   . . . climb to the top of the tower, where you give a long-winded speech about how superheroes are a cancer on this world, and you are the only cleansing agent that can eradicate their vile stench. Then, you go home and masturbate.

F. . . . sneak your way into the heroes' trophy room, where you grab all their old pictures of themselves hugging each other. You forge their signatures on them and sell the photos on eBay for a pretty penny.

G. . . . try to kill everyone and everything in sight while you prattle on and on about how this is the "natural order of the universe."

If you chose option A, you are power-mad.

If you chose option B, you are a bloodluster.

If you chose option C, you are a revengencer.

If you chose option D, you are an I'll-show-them-o-mancer.

If you chose option E, you are a villain fetishist, and we don't want to shake your hand.

If you chose option F, you are money-hungry.

If you chose option G, you are damned insane.

Chapter 4

Persona[*]

---

* Chapter 4 is sponsored by MOLT 'N WEAR, "Fashionable female apparel for people who have suddenly turned into half-lobsters—better than butter and lemon juice!"

The halls in our hive-like underground headquarters are covered with fliers displaying the acronym "WAGIYAN," which stands for "Without a Great Identity, You Are Nothing." We had nothing to do with them, but The Motivatron, the living brain of a shamed motivational speaker implanted into the stomach of a fifteen-foot-tall robot, insisted we put them up or threatened to hold a no-breaks, nine-month seminar about how to unlock your inner monster . . . so we relented. (Incidentally, in the henchman barracks, "wagiyan" has become a slang term for the process of shoving one or more testicles into someone's nostril.)

In spite of the overwhelming obnoxiousness of ubiquitous, inspirational posters, the sentiment holds true. In supervillainy, image is everything. Experience, education, and a foolproof plan can get you a long way in this game, but without a unique, head-turning persona and a bombastic presence, even the most capable villain is just another guy breaking into an embassy with a forty-foot energy sword.

So before you start sewing together your armored body suit, take some time to think about exactly how you want to be viewed in the supervillain and superhero community, because you're going to be stuck with whatever you come up with for pretty much the rest of your career. It's like a band name. Do you think Hootie and the Blowfish still want to be Hootie and the Blowfish? No. No they don't. But they came up with that name one night, presumably while high on turpentine, and had to spend the next several years of success, plus, the following lifetime's worth of obscurity living it down.

To make sure you don't become a supervillain equivalent of Hootie and the Blowfish, we present the following rundown of the key aspects of your supervillain identity.

Name

Some of us luck out. With a last name like von Doom, Horrible, Scorpio, Oblivion, or Murderknife, our monikers are laid out for us from the get-go (and it's kind of hard to go into accounting). Others get the benefit of a pitch-perfect, horrifying nickname. Like, one of our members got the name The Brain Butcher when he was in high school. We're not sure how he got that title, but we have our guesses. (They all involve butchering brains.)

Most supervillains don't get that luxury. In large part, they're saddled with birth names like Mike Wordsworth and Sandra Mixon, like most other workaday shlubs out there punching a clock to make their daily dime. For them, the naming process is a little more difficult, but they also have more freedom to create the evil image they think suits them best.

If you weren't blessed (cursed) with an automatic villain name at birth, keep these tips in mind as you develop your hellish handle:

- Keep it close to your real name if you can. Say, for instance, your name is Ray Mantara. It's not that much of a stretch for you to stick a tail on yourself and become the Viciously Stinging Manta Ray. If your name's Roxy Smith, then consider becoming Lady Rock-Smith (you may also want to learn how to forge rocks into spears and horseshoes and stuff).

- Avoid duplication. Frankly, we don't give a shit about copyright law and all that garbage (though if we see any illegal copies of this book floating around on file-sharing sites, we will move quickly forward with our plans to destroy the internet by ridding the world of kitten pictures). No, our concern here has more to do with avoiding confusion than anything else. Look, we can't have two Jokers running around; unless that's part of a villainous plan he's got going where an impostor creates distractions while he wreaks havoc on Gotham or something. But outside of that circumstance, we try to avoid confusing the heroes (and they confuse easily), the media, and each other as much as possible. So if you absolutely cannot live without doing a clown shtick, look into becoming Jocular Jones or Clownicus or something like that. It'll just make everyone's life so much easier.

- Fit your shtick. Simply: If you're completely hairless and you shoot fireballs out of your fingertips, then The Terrible Timberwolf isn't the name for you.

- Remember brevity. Heroes aren't going to want to spend their time on you if, whenever they confront you, they have to say something like, "Stand down, Onerous, Obstructionist Orphan Oliver, Now-adult Protagonist of the Charles Dickens Book!" A name like that takes away from valuable fighting time. Plus, superheroes aren't all that good with polysyllabic words. So, for the sake of your own fame and to avoid having to tell oafs with greasy hair how to pronounce your nom de plume, go with something simple, like "Evil Oliver Twist," and be done with it.

Powers/Expertise

Most supervillains don't get a say in this part of their personae. But, if you do get that chance, like, say, you get to choose what powers you get as a subject of extensive, yet surprisingly democratic, government testing, then go for something unique and different. (We'll discuss this topic more in Chapter 6.)

SUPERVILLAIN HISTORY FACT

Three U.S. presidents of the 20th century were, in fact, supervillains. Many believe that Richard Nixon was one of them. That is not true. Nixon was a henchman put into power by a cabal of supervillains who irrationally hated circular hotels. The three genuine supervillain presidents were: William Howard Taft (villain name: The Deathtub), Franklin D. Roosevelt (villain name: Poliolus), and Ronald Reagan (villain name: Oven Dutch).

Methods

Your ultimate goal in villainy (see previous chapter) will obviously play some part in determining what type of supervillain you are, but you're also largely defined by the methods you use to achieve those goals. In fact, the six types of supervillain are chiefly defined by method:

1. *The Conqueror*

As the name implies, this villain is a ruthless power player who will use direct force to get what he or she wants. Often, he or she will use alien armies, flying tanks, giant gas bombs, or assemblages of other villains to perform his or her dastardly, usually large-scale acts. Don't be fooled, though: This villain may not be in it only for power. Sometimes, the Conqueror simply likes to stomp as many people under his or her heel as possible, just for the hell of it.

2. *The Mastermind*

The Mastermind's goals are often identical to those of the Conqueror, but he or she is more subtle in methodology. What amounts to an entire criminal plan for some villains serve as mere distractions, complications or kinks in the grand, drawn-out master plans of the Mastermind. Often, Mastermind plans take years to carry out. Sometimes, they'll hire the Thug or the Wild Card to carry out one part of their plan, while a minion carries out another portion elsewhere. Precision and caution are key, despite the fact that some superheroes will almost certainly swoop in and punch it all away, right as it's coming to fruition.

3. *The Madman*

Here's how you define the Madman's methods: The Madman is impossible to define. One thing you can pretty much guarantee, though, is that whatever he's going to do, it'll be scary as hell. He (or if a madwoman, she) will always surprise you with how extraordinarily violent, sick, and dangerous he or she can be. Often they desire only violence and destruction, but sometimes they love money or seek power. You can never really tell with those crazy fools.

4. *The Wild Card*

Not to be confused with the Madman, the Wild Card has very clear goals, and, by all appearances, seems to be a well-adjusted individual. However, his or her loyalties are often fleeting, and they will regularly stab anyone in the back in order to get what they want, which is often money, but could also be other things as well; such as the keys to a bank where they can steal a lot of money. Often handsome, dashing, fast-talkers, Wild Cards are the very definition of douchiness.

5. *The Thug*

The thug does one thing very well: Pound on superheroes (or anyone else who might need a pounding). But just because brute force is his or her stock in trade, the Thug is not necessarily a moron (although many seem to be). He or she is often loyal, though it's not unheard of for a Thug to turn on a Mastermind or even a Conqueror for his or her own personal gain. Often, they do this by trying to pound said Mastermind or Conqueror into submission.

6. *The Trickster*

One might say the Trickster is essentially a neutered version of the Madman, but that is to underestimate the Trickster. Yes, both may laugh often and wear colorful outfits, but the Trickster, like the Mastermind, has very specific goals in mind when he or she places clues at the scene of a crime for a superhero or affixes the police commissioner to the handle of a giant jack-in-the-box. Also, the Trickster is less interested in killing than the Madman. Often, he or she simply wants to best everyone else in a match of wits, but has lost his or her Trivial Pursuit game in the back of the closet.

PROFILES IN LAME SUPERVILLAINY

Typeface

History: War veteran Gordon Thomas became a sign maker after his wife left him. But when another guy bought the company he worked for, he got all upset and became a supervillain. So, to recap: wife leaves you, go find a job making signs; lose sign-making job, become a supervillain. Thomas drew letters all over his body with a grease pen and dubbed himself Typeface, because in addition to reacting to things inappropriately, he also lacks creativity, which could account for why he got fired as a sign maker.

M.O.: Thomas attacks the new owner of the sign-making business and Spider-Man (who is involved for some reason) with the giant letters he apparently stole from the place where he used to work, again displaying his less-than-desirable attributes as an employee. In a true display of lameness, he is defeated not by Spider-Man but by the fellow who bought the business, when the guy sets off a bomb destroying the building he had just bought. So essentially no superhero was necessary in the story of a bad, disgruntled employee and what is clearly a terrible businessman.

Attire

Your clothes, especially if they cover any and all facial features and exposed skin (and we recommend that), are the first things that most people will notice about you. That is, until you become a national legend whose mere name sparks instant fear and pant-urination to the teeming masses. But again, one thing at a time.

You must make sure that your clothing matches your villainous style and the image you want to put across. You have some leeway with what you want to wear, but certain fashion choices are outright no-no's for certain villain types. (For example, it's pretty much a no-no for a male villain to wear anything a female villain would wear.) The helpful chart below will clue you in to what you should and shouldn't be wearing.

	Best for . . .	Not for . . .	Professional Tip
Battle armor / military uniform	The Thug, The Conqueror, The Wild Card	The Mastermind, The Madman, The Trickster	Best (worst) for villains who will be in the field, crushing skulls.
Spandex or leather	The Mastermind, The Trickster, The Thug, The Madman, The Wild Card	The Conqueror	Standard dress, but keep in mind that it's sometimes hard to be menacing with your junk showing.
Business suit	The Mastermind, The Conqueror, The Trickster	The Madman, The Thug, The Wild Card	For when you're attempting to give the appearance of "legitimacy."
Brightly colored, ill-fitting suit	The Madman, The Wild Card, The Trickster	The Thug, The Mastermind, The Conqueror	A good (bad) indicator that you don't give a shit about "legitimacy."

	Best for . . .	Not for . . .	Professional Tip
Street clothes	The Trickster, The Thug, The Wild Card	The Conqueror, The Mastermind, The Madman	People won't remember just a t-shirt and jeans, so try to make your ensemble as ugly and memorable as possible.
Lab coat and goggles	The Mastermind, The Wild Card, The Madman	The Thug, The Conqueror, The Wild Card	For when you want it to look like you actually invent stuff rather than making henchmen do all your R & D.
Nothing	The Thug, The Wild Card	The Trickster, The Madman, The Conqueror, The Mastermind	Appropriate only for animal-hybrid villains, those with no genitals, and characters in Heavy Metal.

Please don't go nude.

Once you've picked your type of attire, you're going to want to answer three remaining questions regarding your super-villain look:

1. Mask or no mask?

To answer this question, ask yourself another: Would I want my mother knowing I was flying around on a personal gliding device, heaving bombs shaped like skulls at men with bug powers? If your mother wouldn't care, then don't worry about it. If she would, then you'd better go with the mask. If you killed your own mother, then it probably doesn't make much of a difference. Go with your gut, or with her ghost, who regularly speaks to you.

2. Cape or no cape?

If you saw the startlingly inaccurate propaganda film, *The Incredibles*, you may think capes are just an accident waiting to happen, what with all the gruesome imagery of cape-wearing people getting sucked into plane engines and such. But we have a counterpoint to that argument. Sometimes, they look really cool; especially when they've got awesome hoods and stuff. So if you want to look awesome, you're probably going to want to look into getting a cape.

3. What about a logo on my chest or belt buckle?

This one depends on a few variables. Are you willing to put a giant target on yourself simply so that everyone can know all about your nuclear-based superpowers or that your name begins with an R? In most cases, the answer will be yes.

Completing the Circle: Picking a Nemesis

Now that you've mostly completed the process of developing your supervillain persona, there's one thing left to do to cement your identity, and that's picking the superhero who best fits your unique style of menace. Keep the following tips in mind when picking the superhero or superheroes you plan to torment for the majority of your career (some cross-over is allowed, but only with prior approval), so you don't get stuck with someone you might end up being friends with or something.

- Find your opposite number
  If there happens to be a superhero out there who has the same powers as you—that is, they're the good version of you, or if he or she has the opposite powers as you, then they're pretty much tailor-made for you, dogg. Speaking of dogs, it's also neat if you can find a hero with whom you can recreate natural enmities. So if you're The Rott-Wilder, then you should seek out Tabby Terrific, like, now.

- Avoid those who would neutralize you
  We know that you want to find your thematic adversary, but it's just plain stupid to go toe-to-toe with superheroes who basically cancel you out. Like, if your powers are based solely on getting people to believe the things you say are true, then you're probably not going want to have any battles with Mr. Existential. And don't get me started talking about the time The Volt tussled with Hydrant Man. There was steam and squirrel carcasses everywhere.

- Think long and hard about taking on a team
  Superheroes team up way more than villains do, and some of them only come as a combo package.

  <u>Pros:</u> Variety. The possibility that they'll get into an argument with each other and you won't even have to do anything. Members are considerably more disposable.

  <u>Cons:</u> Punching from six or seven rather than one. Banter. Severe henchman loss.

- Match your aptitude

If you're an incredibly powerful monarch seeking to assume control over entire continents or planets, then you may want to aim higher than an aging acrobat with no superpowers and a biting wit. Likewise, it may be a good idea for you not to take on nigh-omnipotent, invulnerable types if you're an embezzler who lifts weights sometimes.

- Personal is better
  Think back over the course of your life. At any point, did you do anything that may have created a superhero? Or did a superhero do anything that might have caused you to go into villainy? If so, find them, have a little reunion, then beat the shit out of each other.

Chapter 5

Rhetoric*

I can't stress this enough. Talk constantly.

---

* Chapter 5 is sponsored by RAY GUNN'S SIZZLIN' STEAKHOUSE, "We are
not officially affiliated with supervillains or ray guns, despite the unfortunate
name of our owner."

As I have so powerfully demonstrated in the four chapters leading up to this one (and will continue to demonstrate until the day I become some kind of man-god who is no longer restrained by the shackles of language), is that sometimes, the word can be your deadliest weapon, my dear evil reader. Ah, but the question lies as how best (worst) to sharpen that acid tongue? How can you utilize the power of the larynx to decimate the ever-growing legions of goodness and light with precision, mastery, and the maximum amount of destructive force?

To answer those questions, here we have a few things to tell you and say about what you can do so you can talk real good (bad) and mention right words such as how we do talk.

What to Say

You can pretty much say whatever you want, as long as it's commanding, blustery, sounds cool, and is preferably, alliterative; puns are appropriate too. Preferably, use the type that causes people to cringe violently. (Example: "Puns are a-pun-priate, too.")

While it's crucial to know what to say, it's far more important to be aware of what *not* to say. Some things that you'll feel compelled to expel from your mouth because it's "standard practice," or because you want to fit in with the villaingentsia are just plain outdated. And while we supervillains are probably the group of people most likely to embrace cliché (death rays will never get old to us), even we have to admit when something is old.

A few examples of what you really should avoid:

- "This ends here!"
  It sounds cool, sure, and it gives the inexperienced the impression that you're in control. But what if, somehow, you end up teleporting to Malaysia or something during the course of the fight? (This actually happens more often than you might think.) It will not have ended there, and you'll end up looking quite foolish.

- "We're not so different, you and I."
  Of course you're not. You and your superhero counterpart are both people who have chosen to bounce around a major city in an outfit that chafes. You've obviously got more similarities than differences, and are probably both clinically insane. So why point it out? Yeah, it's an effective gambit to butter up superheroes into feeling sympathy for you before you strike, but come up with something better to say than this repetitive old fallback.

- "And I would have gotten away with it, too, if it hadn't been for you meddling kids!"
  Stop giving them so much damn credit! All you're doing is stroking their egos, and those meddling kids don't need any more confidence. Plus, odds are you were going to figure out a way to screw this up without them, Old Man Harrison. You haven't been able to take over the old amusement park up to now. What makes you think that would change?

- "Nobody move!"
  This command just doesn't work. It never fails that when you come bursting into a bank, and yell out a "nobody move!" that someone will try to play hero and press an

alarm or come after you with a shotgun. It's better to adhere to the strategy of flooding the whole building with a paralyzing gas beforehand and saying something cool and thematic like, "I have come to take out a lifetime no-interest loan consisting of all your money. Pray I don't make your lives collateral."

- "Who dares challenge (your name here)?"
  It sounds ominous, I'll grant you that. But it's also just an evil-sounding way to say, "My name is _____, what's yours?" Like some kind of bad-guy name-tag greeting.

- "Welcome . . . to your DOOM!"
  Welcome is too polite a word for use in most supervillain endeavors. Courtesy is not generally the way to go. It's like saying "Thank you . . . for dying!" It just makes you sound schizophrenic and campy.

- "Nooooooooooo!"
  No.

More examples of overused supervillain catchphrases, all of which are linked with particular villains of wide renown, are listed at the end of this chapter.

SUPERVILLAIN HISTORY FACT

Joseph Barbera, one half of the supervillain cartoon making duo Hanna-Barbera, devised a plan in the 1950s to hypnotize children into buying cheap plastic toys, the money from which they then planned to use to buy various doomsday devices and pour into superhero destruction. The plan was this: Create cartoons in which cats chased mice in front of a background which constantly repeated. That repeating background was the key to the hypnotism scheme, and won Barbera many super-villain awards. His plan continues successfully to this day.

When to Say It

As a general rule, you should talk all the time . . . even when no one else is around, keep talking, as you never know when your exploits might be recorded in a comic book (yes, they're propaganda rags, but we have to take what publicity we can get), and those readers are going to need expository dialogue to know what's going on. Plus, being strong and silent is more of a hero thing. We're not into that. We're more slippery, lumpy, and chatty.

Your logorrhea should be unceasing for sure, but your manner of speech and what you say may change depending on the circumstances in which you find yourself. Some common situations you may have to deal with:

- When confronted with a superhero
  Load them up with threats, curse their insolence, harp on how badly they will fail, creatively use the word "destruction."

- When addressing henchmen
  Constantly dress them down, question their abilities, undermine their confidence, command them to do things they can't or won't possibly do. (More on this in Chapter 7.)

- When talking to other villains
  Incessantly reiterate that your genitals are larger than theirs, yell about your credentials, exchange stories about idiot henchmen.

- When placing a hero into a death trap
  Run through the details of your plot because they'll be dead soon and you've been dying to tell someone. Discuss the brilliance of your foolproof death trap, laugh with verve.

- After the superhero escapes your death trap
  Curse unyieldingly

- When being dragged away to jail by a superhero police or other authorities
  Make creative use of the phrases "you'll pay for this" and "next time," laugh menacingly, making sure to announce your escape plan.

- When being interrogated while in prison
  Tell your origin story, give a cryptic but ultimately helpful clue for apprehending a rival villain, ensure that your vendetta against the hero doing the interrogating stands with a standard-issue "It's not over between me and you."

Where to Say It

As I am sure I have made it abundantly clear by now, you should talk everywhere you go. At your headquarters, at the superhero's hideout, in jail, at the bank, in the shower, while you're on trial, in your sleep, at the library, while you take over the studio at the local TV station, anywhere you go disguised as someone else, in space, when you go to visit your parents, at your best friend's house, in hell, in your cyberspace lair, at a public park, at day cares, and just about anywhere else, you should be talking.

The only places where you shouldn't talk are those places where you physically cannot speak, like in an operating room where your voice box has been removed or some other dimension where there's no sound. But even there, you should keep trying.

PROFILES IN LAME SUPERVILLAINY

Big Wheel

History: Jackson Wheele was a businessman who just happened to be embezzling from his own company. After the (lame) villain Rocket Racer blackmails him, he acquires a costume made of a giant mechanical wheel chases Rocket Racer in a lame-off across New York City.

M.O.: Spider-Man eventually got involved, but, as you might expect, the guy drove himself right into a river, because his entire body was in a giant wheel. Lesson: It's probably best to know how to operate your stupid machinery before using it.

Who to Say it to

There's only one group of people you should never talk to, and that's those assholes at the Worldwide Conglomeration of Super Criminals. They deserve exactly zero percent of your attention. Say nothing to them. Nothing.

Got it?

How to Say It

The best way to say what you need to say is to open your mouth (or mouths, depending on what kind of mutations/deformities/alien body-melding you've got going on), vibrate your vocal cords, and adjust your tongue, lips, and teeth to form words accordingly.

Beyond that, I suggest that you keep your volume high, your tone deep, and your letters in ALL CAPS.

It's also important to make sure that you punctuate at least every other sentence with an evil and/or menacing laugh. Keep in mind that only a few laughs are truly evil. Here's a quick rundown of some laughs you should and shouldn't use.

- Ha-ha-ha-ha-ha!—A little boring, but okay.
- HAhaHAHaHaHAhahAHA!—Better.
- Tee-hee-hee!—Avoid.
- Huh-huh. A-huhuhuhuhuh.—Too henchman-y.
- One of those laughs where you open your mouth and grab your belly, but no sound comes out.—Too avuncular.
- Har-har-harrrr: Sarcastic. Workable, if that's your thing.
- Hennnh-hennnh-hennnnnnnnnnh—Creepy. A worthwhile choice.
- Haw-haw-haw!—There are worse choices, especially useful if you're some kind of mountain man.
- A rhythmic hiss—Only appropriate for reptilian villains and hench-dogs.
- Bwa-hahahahaha!—Never, ever "bwa."
- Mwa-hahahahaha!—Perfect.

Ten Supervillains Who Need New Catchphrases

These famous, comic-book starring guys (and girls) have some of the most played-out catchphrases in the history of villaindom. Don't be like them.

1. Doctor Sivana (Captain Marvel's arch-nemesis)

Catchphrase: "Curses! Foiled again!"

Why it's a problem: Let's look past the fact that it's a phrase that has become the biggest supervillain cliche ever, and get right down to the heart of the matter. This is a catchphrase based on **failure**. For it to be known as one's catchphrase, then, is to imply that that person is always going to fail, and expects to do so. It pegs the speaker as a loser and a defeatist. That's no way to go through life. Plus, what do you do if you actually win one? You have nothing to say. So, Doctor Sivana, I propose that you find a new lease on life and begin loudly shouting, "I won!" even if you're beaten so badly that you'll have to eat and breathe through tubes for a month. You'll feel better, and people will remember you as a winner, even though, let's face it, you aren't.

2. Venom (Spider-Man's arch-nemesis)

Catchphrase: "We are Venom!"

Why it's a problem: Look, it's fine to introduce yourself by your supervillain handle after the accident that makes you into a man-eating creature of living goop or even upon your first encounter with your arch-nemesis, but after that, well, it just comes off as kind of self-indulgent and, frankly, redundant. Yes, we know you're Venom. Why not use those ever-important pre-battle moments for saying something that will really have an effect on your nemesis rather than just reminding him of your name, you know, in case he forgot the name of the opposite number who's bugging him, like, every week? Might we suggest, "Up yours, Parker?"

3. General Zod (Superman villain)

Catchphrase: "Kneel before Zod!"
Why it's a problem: If it existed purely in a vacuum, there would be nothing wrong with this supervillain catchphrase. It's got a pitch-perfect level of arrogance mixed in with domination of subordinates and clear delusions of grandeur. It even manages to get his name in there without seeming forced (take note, Venom). No, this is a case, like with many okay-to-good movies and bands, where the fans ruined it. As soon as "Kneel before Zod" became the battle cry of message-board nerds who thought themselves the winner of a forum argument, it was dead. So very dead.

4. Galactus (Professional planet eater)

Catchphrase: "I hunger!"
Why it's a problem: Well, it's certainly not too wordy. No, this catchphrase seems to suffer from the opposite problem: It sounds like something a toddler would say.

And that would be fine if Galactus was supposed to be some kind of giant intergalactic infant like the one at the end of "2001," going around eating planets. But he isn't. He's "the most awesome living entity in the cosmos," according to the Hero/Villain Bible (a comic book). You'd think, then, he could manage something a little more erudite than three syllables, shouted loudly.

5. The Riddler (Batman villain)

Catchphrase: "Riddle me this . . . "
Why it's a problem: Simply, it doesn't make any damn sense. I know it's supposed to be an original twist on "answer me this" or "solve these riddles three" or whatever, but riddle just isn't a verb. At least, not in the sense that the Riddler tries to use it. I mean, you can riddle someone with bullets or even with riddles, but never, ever (or at least not in the last couple centuries) has the word riddle meant, "the act of solving a riddle." Even if it was a verb in that context, wouldn't it mean, like, asking a riddle? . . . My head hurts.

6. Dr. Claw (Inspector Gadget's arch-nemesis)

Catchphrase: "I'll get you next time, Gadget . . . next time!"
Why it's a problem: While Dr. Claw avoids the pitfall of the aforementioned Dr. Sivana, there is one big flaw here. This is what we call a "dependent catchphrase." That is to say, it relies on the existence of another character, usually a hero (in this

case, Inspector Gadget). Dependent catchphrases are awfully limiting, in that they tend to only allow villains to face off against one hero and no one else. What's especially bad about this one is the assumption that there will, in fact, be a next time, with the implication that Dr. Claw expects another 30-minute gag-fest in which an incompetent cyborg, a young girl, and a bipedal, mute dog best him, when he probably should simply be considering ways to burn their house down one night and get the whole thing over with.

7. The Blob (X-Men villain)

Catchphrase: "Nothing can move the Blob!"
Why it's a problem: It is patently, on-its-face false. Sure, it's difficult to gain enough momentum to topple the Blob. It may even be tough for the average Joe to acquire the leverage to lift him up or push him forward. But something can absolutely move him. I mean, he can walk, right? So the Blob **can move himself**. No other test is needed. Something can, in fact, move the blob. Case closed.

8. Hydra (Super-terrorist group)

Catchphrases: "Hail Hydra!"
    "Cut off one head, and two more will take its place"

Why they're a problem: It's confusing. What exactly are they hailing? Themselves? Their leader, Madame Hydra? The mythical creature with nine heads? Hell if I know. As for their other phrase, it's an appropriate, if maybe a little-too-on-the-nose, allusion to the mythical Hydra. But boy, it's a mouthful, isn't it? Would it be too much to sacrifice literary reference for directness? "You cannot defeat us!" seems like it would get the point across pretty well.

9. Harley Quinn (Batman villain)

Catchphrase: "Mistah J"

Why it's a problem: This is another example of the dependent catchphrase, but of a different variety. Where Dr. Claw's relies on the existence of a hero, this one is dependent on the existence of a so-called "boss villain," forever locking in the speaker as a "number two." So if the young Ms. Quinn ever wants to set out on her own in this white-knuckle, claw-your-way-to-the-top business we call villainy, she'd better find something new.

10. Juggernaut (X-Men villain)

Catchphrase: "Nothing can stop the Juggernaut"

Why it's a problem: To quickly debunk phrase No. 1: The Juggernaut can stop himself, therefore the phrase is not true. Although it does make one wonder what would happen if an "unstoppable" force (Juggernaut) met an "immovable" object (Blob).

Why you Should Talk

Because it is *our* way. We are villains. We monologue. So if you've got hang-ups when it comes to public speaking, you may want to go into something more suited to your talents, like becoming a human doormat.

Training Exercise 3: Breath Control

With all the talking we villains do, it's pretty necessary that you learn how to master your lungs. Like an opera singer, a supervillain pours music out of his or her mouth. But our music doesn't have a tune or rhythm or anything like that. Instead, it's mostly just talking about crushing people's spirits and finally getting our vengeance and lingering for a really long time on the word "WOOOOOOORRRRLD."

But other than those minor differences, it's just like opera.

And not unlike some great tenor or soprano, it's imperative that you are able to hold out your notes (or, in our case, threats) for what seems like minutes at a time. Try the following exercise to get to the point where you can monologue and monologue and no one notices that you even ever breathe.

Repeat the following:

"Insolent fools! You have walked right into my nefarious trap! You should have known that this old castle in a warehouse was once my family homestead, and now it just happens to be located inside a building owned by the scientific research and development firm that so flippantly fired me some five years ago! And now, giant spikes made of fire and with man-eating crocodiles attached to the ends will very slowly descend, upon you so that you will eventually be impaled, cooked, and digested over the course of the next several hours. But that's not the only way you will soon be dying, you do-gooding meddlers! Radioactive acid will also soon begin rising out of the floor, surrounding your feet to the ankle, dissolving you into a pool of gamma-irradiated bubbly water. So, basically, in summary: Your top half will be sliced, burned, and eaten. Your lower half will be melted while also receiving a flash-case of radiation poisoning. Now, I'll be leaving to go do some things I need to do that are apparently more important than staying here and watching you, the arch-nemesis I have devoted my entire life to defeating, die. Enjoy your demise! Mwa-hahahahahahahahaha!"

* * *

Continue to repeat this monologue at least once a day until you can complete it in one breath, at most. If you can get to that point, you're definitely ready for the field. For bonus points and added atmosphere, put a superhero in the exact death trap described each time you practice.

Chapter 6

Abilities/ Equipment*

You can never have enough pouches.

---

* Chapter 6 is sponsored by AXES 'R US, "We are literally sentient axes. Our lives are nothing but pain."

A question I've been hearing virtually non-stop through the Psychomonitor since pretty much page one, but that I chose not to answer until just now because I like keeping you in suspense is, "can I become a supervillain if I don't have any superpowers?"

The short answer is yes, you can absolutely become a supervillain if you don't have any superpowers. (Several prominent villains have demonstrated that very fact and are listed at the end of this chapter.) But know this: If you try to go into a gun battle with a knife, you're going to lose. Similarly, if you go into a fight with superheroes, and you don't have any inborn powers, the biggest brain on the continent, chemically-induced superhuman abilities, or some kind of device that gives you a fighting chance against a guy who can shoot heat beams out of his eyes, then you're pretty much going to get stomped. It'll be less like a knife in a gunfight than a pebble in a missile-launching competition.

With that in mind, how best (worst) to go toe-to-toe with the overpowered, under-intelligent superhero contingent? Ingenuity, my dear friends. Ingenuity.

Bringing Superpowers to You

So, you weren't born with superpowers? You don't work in a place that manufactures, stores, or distributes nuclear waste? You aren't a scientist who, for reasons known to no one but you, only ever uses yourself as a test subject? You don't know any wizards or aliens fond of distributing super-power-granting rings?

Not to worry, you don't need to have any of those (admittedly useful) connections, as there are other ways to get superpowers.

Namely, you can buy them from us for three low, low payments of $39,999.99. We will have you go through an agonizing series of isolation-chamber procedures that will grant you a superpower (or for just $10,000 more, any combination of two) from a list of twenty-one high-quality powers found at the end of this chapter.

If you are too dirt-poor to buy our high-quality powers (hey, you gotta spend money to make money, folks), you could alternately try:

- Taking a lot of different drugs at one time and seeing what happens.
- Spending your nights in the desert and hoping that an alien notices you.
- Praying to some gods, Satan, Cthulhu.
- Repeatedly telling yourself you have powers and just hoping that it happens.
- Killing people who do have powers and seeing if you absorb theirs as a reward.
- Doing something really noble and seeing what that gets you (it's totally easy to use those powers for evil even if you earned them from doing good).
- Trying to talk a goat or some other animal into fusing itself with your DNA.
- Asking for powers for Christmas/Hanukkah/Kwanzaa (it helps if your relatives are supervillains/superheroes/mad scientists/gods/Satan/Cthulhu).
- Standing around in various hazardous waste storage facilities.

- Getting bitten by various things, especially if they've been irradiated or genetically altered.
- Hanging around superheroes a lot, getting in their way, otherwise generally playing off their tendency to create supervillains.
- Trying out various chants involving the words "might," "power," "demon," "stones," "runes," "magic," "sword," "dark," "blood," "moon," "Jupiter," "pentagram," "shambolic," "tatters," "terrible," "black out the earth's sun."

SUPERVILLAIN HISTORY FACT

Marlene Dietrich was the first openly supervillain actress in Hollywood. She kept her supervillainy secret for much of her career, but was outed as a villainess in 1942, when she was spotted on top of a studio water tower, remote controlling a robot replica of John Wayne on the set of the film "The Spoilers." At the time, the robot John Wayne was beating up several hundred studio midgets.

Going Without

If you for some reason don't want to give the International Society of Supervillains' R & D department your life savings and none of those other top-notch suggestions work out for you, you may want to completely avoid the whole superhuman game and simply try to obtain and use peak human skills. Examples of this are things like genius-level intelligence, Olympic strength, record-setting speed, cat-like agility, Bruce Lee-style kung fu prowess, the ability to talk really fast like the guy from the old Micro Machines commercials, unbelievable crocheting skills, et cetera.

Of course, to reach levels of peak human skill, you're going to have to do a lot of training—near-constant training—from pretty much birth. So hopefully, you're reading this in-utero. (We hope to publish a book-on-placenta right around the time we go into our next printing.)

If not, you may have to look into other methods, such as . . .

Technology: The enemy of your enemy (a.k.a., your friend)

You don't have to do any of the annoying shit it takes to acquire superpowers or gain incredible athletic abilities or incredible brilliance as long as you know the right (wrong) people. And by "the right people," of course, I mean people from whom you can steal super-boss gizmos that let you do what any tights-wearing superhero can do by, like, tomorrow.

But what gizmos are best (worst) to get your hands on? I, the author of a book about being a professional super-villain, just so happens to have the answers for you. (Who would have thought!) Next time your employer lets you into his or her super-secret room full of experimental test equipment, keep your eyes open for:

- Jet-propelled gliders and/or jet packs
  Perfect for causing free-form aerial terror as efficiently as possible.

- Cybernetic battle suits
Bonus points if said suits include capabilities of increasing or decreasing size, invisibility, invulnerability, stretchiness, or incessantly blinking lights.

- Gauntlets of various types
They should shoot out something awesome, like napalm or solid ice or other awesome gauntlets.

- Mind-control helmets
The easiest way to steal these is to acquire a helmet that blocks mind control beforehand.

- Time machines
If not invented yet, wait until one is invented, steal it, and then bring it to your younger self for more immediate use.

- Robots, animals or robot animals
Also useful are magic animals that can teleport and shit.

- Teleportation devices
In the event that you can't find any magic animals.

- Huge computers
For making giant schematics, viewing large images of superheroes going through death traps, bringing a certain ambience to a headquarters, et cetera. Also, for doing humongous word processing.

- Aging or de-aging devices

For when you're too young to be taken seriously or too old to wait out that time machine.

- Any type of ray
  Death, freeze, heat, disintegrator, knockout, manta, pulse. But I especially recommend the CR-9666 Death's Head Revolution, a knockout ray that won't take up your whole atrium.

- Any type of gas
  Poison, radioactive, nerve, noxious, laughing, knockout, poo, erotic. But especially poison.

PROFILES IN LAME SUPERVILLAINY

Terra-Man
History: After an alien killed Toby Manning's father, the alien took the young man in and raised him as his own. Once Toby grew up, he killed the alien and returned to Earth, adopting the name Terra-Man because, no joke, he was from Earth.

M.O.: When he killed his alien-Dad, Manning stole a big store of advanced alien technology that just happened to resemble the six-shooters and lassos and whatnot of the Old West. He also got a winged horse from somewhere. With those things and a ridiculous-looking cloak and cowboy hat, he fights Superman. Yes. Superman. With a high-tech lasso.

Smoke and Mirrors (Literally)

One great thing about superheroes is how easily confused they are—seriously. You can just throw down one gas pellet, zoom around a corner, jump behind a dumpster, and they'll think you've up and disappeared like some kind of magic man. That sort of beautiful gullibility makes things a lot easier for us villains, since we tend to have to make a lot of escapes and running isn't really our thing.

So it couldn't hurt to learn a thing or two about special effects.

Let's say, for example, that you've been confronted with a superhero that can't leave well enough alone and let you sabotage the extraordinarily large ferris wheel at the amusement park by the shore in peace. All you have to do is lead him or her on a trail to a hall of mirrors and give the superhero the impression that he or she has clocked you good, when, in fact, they just broke one of the carnival's most impressive and expensive mirrors. (They'll never pay for it either, even when made aware of the fact that all they succeeded in doing was ruining a hard-working mirrorsmith's life work. Heroes break more stuff than we ever will, and still get all the acclaim, and yet another example of the hero-industrial complex.) They'll leave you alone and all you had to do was take a quick fall and sell it.

Then, you'll be free to go take an uninterrupted whiz in the caramel they dip the apples in before getting back out your giant wrench.

21 Common Superpowers: Pros and Cons

Flight

Pros: Little to no traffic; easy access to planes and helicopters which you can threaten; allows you to keep up with flying heroes (which are common).

Cons: Easy to be mistaken for a superhero; constant bugs and birds in your face; if it craps out on you, you're in trouble.

Invulnerability

Pros: No need to worry about superheroes' constant punching; if another supervillain tries to stab you (which is going to happen), then you can have a good laugh about it instead of dying.

Cons: You can't feel it when it hurts so good (and by that we mean during sex); germs can get in, but intravenous drugs can't.

Invisibility

Pros: Going unnoticed by superheroes, cops, other villains, your mom, the entire women's locker room.

Cons: Going unnoticed by just about everyone.

Super Speed

Pros: If you have a reason to go to Malaysia, you can go without having to re-arrange your schedule; you'll rack up at the Olympics.

Cons: You end up going fast everywhere, if you know what I mean (I mean during sex); constantly having to buy new shoes.

Super Strength

Pros: If you can hit them first, you can take puny superheroes down pretty easily; the ability to open any can, any time.

Cons: Car doors come right off; the likelihood that you will probably crush anyone you care about even a little bit.

Stretchiness

Pros: No need for rope when you have an occasion to tie someone up; you can grab things in the other room without having to get off the couch.

Cons: If you happen to pass by an elementary school, kids will play with your arms and legs for hours, and you really won't be able to do much about it.

Superhuman Intelligence

Pros: Bombarding superheroes with math problems makes them virtually helpless; no need to waste your time reading; the ability to win just about any game show other than "Wheel of Fortune," where only dumb luck succeeds.

Cons: Terrible headaches; really difficult to communicate with anybody, especially henchmen, because you only speak in words of seven syllables or more; constantly making people's heads explode with confusion is kind of an inconvenience after the novelty wears off.

Telepathy/Mind Control/Memory Manipulation

Pros: You can make people forget all the assholish crap you do, which is pretty useful at Thanksgiving; less likelihood of getting your hands dirty, since you can get average people or superheroes to do stuff for you.

Cons: Having to hear what everybody thinks about you (especially during sex).

Telekinesis

Pros: If a superhero arrives and you don't want him or her to be there, you can just pick the idiot up and move them or fling a Jeep at them; sandwich-making much less of a hassle.

Cons: Again with the headaches; nosebleeds as well; easy to break stuff if someone says your name, waves boobs in your face or otherwise breaks your concentration.

Teleportation

Pros: Easy escapes; convenient access to various places, such as the women's locker room.

Cons: Getting stuck in walls; getting stuck inside other peoples' bodies; getting stuck in the earth's core; accidentally misplacing a limb.

Size Control

Pros: Ability to turn small provides access to otherwise impenetrable places; ability to turn large provides ability to smash shit.

Cons: Ability to turn small makes you easily crushed or trapped; ability to turn large makes you an easy target and very hard to find stylish attire for.

Time Manipulation

Pros: You can go back in time and kill superheroes before they get their stupid powers; you can go to the future and find out how awesome you'll be.

Cons: Your future and past selves probably won't like you (the assholes); paradoxes are a bitch.

Interdimensional Travel

Pros: Lots and lots of worlds to conquer rather than just the one; infinitely more hideouts.

Cons: You can conquer all the alternate universes you want, but it won't be yours; infinitely more superheroes to bug you.

Healing Factor/Regeneration

Pros: If you have a habit of losing arms and legs, it's not nearly as much of a problem for you; no medical bills; temporary cool scars/wounds with no permanent damage.

Cons: That shit still hurts; you can absorb a lot more bullets, and people are probably going to know that after a few run-ins.

Animal Mimicry

Pros: It would be pretty great to be as ferocious as a lion or fast as a cheetah or to swim like a dolphin.

Cons: What if it malfunctioned and you were permanently stuck on sloth? That'd make things tough.

Control Over Fish/Super Swimming Powers

Pros: Purview over three-fourths of the Earth's surface; the top halves of mermaids.

Cons: Everyone will make fun of you, even with the three-fourths of the surface thing; the bottom halves of mermaids.

Control Over Elements/Metal/Energy

Pros: Projectiles any time you want them; you could build bridges for yourself whenever and wherever you needed them; shooting stuff out of your arms is super-cool.

Cons: As soon as the public notices what you're all about, they'll probably try to harness you for electricity; not good when you lose control of your fire/ice/water/wind/energy/metal (during sex).

Weather Control

Pros: It's always good to be able to call up a storm at the baseball game where the local superhero is supposed to sing the national anthem; making it snow during the summer freaks people out in general; hail is a good (bad) distraction that allows for easy escapes.

Cons: Your only real bargaining chip is causing a drought, and sadly, you still need to drink water, too; impromptu thunderstorms (during sex).

Re-Animation/Bringing Inanimate Objects To Life

Pros: A standing army of zombies or Ottomans available at any time; if friends of yours die, it won't be permanent (though they may try to eat your brain).

Cons: Things that have never lived or have died are really hard to control, and pretty dumb.

Pheromone Production

Pros: You can make people do what you say, and they won't even know why; hot chicks or dudes will be all over you.

Cons: You will smell terrible; ugly chicks or dudes will be all over you, too.

Immortality

Pros: No need to worry about doing life-threatening shit; the benefits of infinite experience.

Cons: Boredom, such terrible, terrible boredom; having to witness the horrors of do-gooders' "progress;" especially if you're into teenage girls, like that *Twilight* vampire.

9 Badass Supervillains Who Don't Have Super Powers

The Joker

Known for: Being Batman's arch nemesis, murder via gas and/or fish, having the largest "HAs" in laughter history.

Why he's a badass: Not only can the guy go toe-to-toe with Batman despite weighing about eighty pounds, the Joker also has an incredible ability to not die. Seriously, I think you could shoot him right in the face, burn his body and dump him in the ocean, he'd still find a way to come back.

If he had a superpower, it would be: Insanity. In fact, DC Comics lists it as a superpower, as if mental states are somehow meta-human; which, if that's the case, I know some people who should suit up and go out as General Anxiety Disorder tomorrow.

The Kingpin

Known for: Being humongous, somehow managing to find dapper suits despite being humongous, ruining Daredevil's life as much as possible.

Why he's a badass: He didn't even have to get his hands dirty to put Matt Murdock, a.k.a. Daredevil, in jail. He got the FBI to do his dirty work for him, getting them to arrest Murdock after convincing them the blind lawyer was Daredevil and promising to give them the non-existent "Murdock Papers." Any supervillain who gets the FBI to do his deeds must have some serious mojo.

If he had a superpower, it would be: He's one of those fat-looking guys who are actually all muscle, so I'm gonna go with super strength.

David Cain

Known for: Being the late-'90s Batgirl's dad, training Batman, being some kind of crazy-awesome assassin.

Why he's a badass: Cain got hired to frame Bruce Wayne for killing his girlfriend, Vesper Fairchild. Why'd he agree to take the job? Because he wanted to see if Batman was worthy of spending time with his daughter, who just happened to be going around town dressed in a Batgirl costume. That's messed up. Also, he has proven that 1) he can escape from prison whenever he wants and 2) he won't die, despite being shot point-blank.

If he had a superpower, it would be: If you can break into Wayne Manor and kill Batman's ladyfriend, then you must be some kind of ghost . . . so ghostery.

Justin Hammer

Known for: Having a really cool name, being a billionaire industrialist, spending his free time screwing things up for fellow billionaire industrialist Iron Man.

Why he's a badass: After finding out he was about to die, Hammer decided he would put off death for a little while, at least, not before ruining Tony Stark and his little wispy mustache. So he built a space station for himself and decided to inject Iron Man with nanites that made him cry like a little girl. Also, the guy has financed approximately eighty- hundred other villains.

If he had a superpower, it would be: The ability to magically conjure money.

Rupert Thorne

Known for: Political corruption, figuring out Batman's secret identity in Batman: The Animated Series.

Why he's a badass: Thorne, not content to simply unsuccessfully torture that little weasel Hugo Strange to figure out Batman's identity, went to great lengths to finally get it by taking some photos of Batman changing costumes from Vicki Vale. Who knew it could be that easy? Also, he had enough sway to start an anti-Batman campaign through the City Council, get his puppet elected mayor, and get Commissioner Gordon fired.

If he had a superpower, it would be: Political acumen, the same superpower that Barack Obama has.

Crossbones

Known for: Wearing a stylish skull mask, occasionally banging the Red Skull's daughter, killing Captain America.

Why he's a badass: Um, he killed Captain America. Okay, so he didn't exactly do it single-handedly, but he did manage to get in the first shot, so that's pretty impressive. And Captain America stayed dead for a good long while, which is more than can be said for the accomplishments of Crossbones' highly super-powered peer, Doomsday (the guy who "killed" Superman), who is actually a total punk.

If he had a superpower, it would be: The ability to laugh while being punched in the face by Bucky.

Lex Luthor

Known for: Baldness, owning a kryptonite ring, managing to retain his position as a legitimate businessman despite being a known criminal who wears brightly colored costumes.

Why he's a badass: He's a regular, bald-headed dude who decides it's a good idea to take on an invincible alien who can burn you to a crisp with his eyes. It seems kind of stupid, but hey, Luthor's gotten some pretty good jabs in on Superman, and even managed to get elected president. Oh, and he was responsible for the entire destruction of Gotham City, which is a pretty big deal.

If he had a superpower, it would be: The ability to return to legitimate business somehow, no matter how many nefarious plots he cooks up.

Cobra Commander

Known for: Regularly yelling "retreat!," running a terrorist organization so confident in its methods that members wear bright red logos on their chests, once being a man.

Why he's a badass: After his former right-hand man shot him in the back, Cobra Commander got a little pissed. Want to know what he did? He basically jumped right out of his grave, imprisoned everybody who had ever pissed him off and buried them under a volcano. Now that's drama. Also, he tried to use cloned dinosaurs to take over the world, as well as giant beams that stole all the gold from Fort Knox.

If he had a superpower, it would be: Raspiness.

Dr. Doom

Known for: Being ridiculously awesome, a stylish metal mask, being really annoyed with Richards.

Why he's a badass: There are about a billion examples here, like when he sent Reed Richards' kids to hell and then showed Richards that he did it via the Fantastic Four's computer; but how about this one: Dr. Doom tricked Dr. Strange into nearly sacrificing himself so that he could free his mother's soul from hell. I can't really say much more than that.

If he had a superpower, it would be: Yes, I know, Doom's armor gives him like eighty powers beyond what a normal human can do, including time travel. But if there was one power innate to Doom, I would have to say it's general kickassitude, if that was a word.[*]

---

[*] (NOTE TO SELF: Kidnap Merriam and Webster, coerce them.)

Chapter 7

Staffing*

Even with all their problems, henchman can
come in pretty handy sometimes.

---

* Chapter 7 is sponsored by THE GLOBAL BROTHERHOOD OF
MISCREANTS, "You will hire us. Oh. You will."

I completely understand the urge to go out into a world full of do-gooders and take on all of herodom, bare-knuckled and full of fire. But it's not the best idea to go at it alone . . . you're going to need some help. Preferably, help that is completely loyal to you and entirely open for even the most ridiculous of suggestions. Help that is more than willing to take a punch, or a kick, or even an elbow to the junk. (Yeah, sometimes, superheroes get real.) Help that's completely expendable, so that when you make your headquarters self-destruct or you need to jump out of a helicopter, you don't have to worry about who you're leaving behind.

That's where henchmen come in.

Yes, a disobedient henchman can be a real pain in the ass, and stupid henchmen are pretty much the constant bane of our existence (though they do a hell of a lot for our ever-important superiority complexes). But, hey, you need them. Somebody's got to build the giant beam that's going to evaporate all the world's water; and you've got important laughing, monologuing, and image managing to do. Plus, we have a working agreement with the Global Brotherhood of Minions to keep their members employed, and one thing even we won't mess with is a union boss.

How Big to Make Your Hench-horde

"Good help is hard to find." That's an old cliché that has more or less turned into an unfunny sitcom punchline.

It's also completely wrong, because it implies that good help actually exists. Good (bad) help is *impossible* to find. That's why it's so important that you hire a veritable army of henchmen to carry out your evil schemes. Among the hundreds or thousands of henchmen you may have on staff, at least one will have to know how to do the tasks you ask of them. Unfortunately, it'll probably only be about one out of every thousand who have any knowledge of things, like fixing your airship or figuring out where the weak point of the superhero headquarters is, or how to set your alarm clock. So it's just smart planning to simply play the odds.

Even if they're all totally clueless, and that is most definitely a possibility, it's at least fun to watch them get crushed as you send wave after wave of them after the superheroes who want to stop you.

SUPERVILLAIN HISTORY FACT

Though widely regarded as a mysterious fluke, Amelia Earhart's disappearance in 1937 was actually the work of a group of early supervillains who identified the plucky young pilot as a superhero in training. To dispatch Ms. Earhart, the villains kidnapped and trained pilot Charles Lindbergh's young son, teaching him the ways of the villain arts. The child (Baby Goodbye) successfully sent Ms. Earhart's plane to another dimension, where it still flies today. Ms. Earhart, meanwhile, struck a deal with Baby Goodbye and conducted villainy with him for many years as Mama Terror.

The crime duo of Baby Goodbye and Mama Terror is responsible for the disappearance of big-band conductor Glenn Miller and Teamsters President Jimmy Hoffa, among many others.

Credentials

There are a number of things you need to make sure your henchmen have on their resumes before you add them to your team. Among those credentials are:

- Respiration
- Skin
- Operating arms and/or legs
- Bones
- Organs

- Four or more working senses

It also helps for them to have:

- The ability to speak
- Elementary-level math skills
- Walking and/or running ability
- Minimal fighting skills or some knowledge of what a fight is

PROFILES IN LAME SUPERVILLAINY

Signalman

History: Phil Cobb nearly got laughed out of town when he came to Gotham City and, with no reputation to speak of, tried to recruit a criminal gang. Dejected, he used his brilliant criminal mind to create a gimmick for his criminal doings based on the road signs he saw people obeying. So he created a bright red and yellow costume covered in symbols because he thought that would stop people from laughing at him.

M.O.: Despite Signalman's signal gimmick, he preferred to commit regular hooligan-style crimes. Unfortunately, his garish costume managed to attract the attention of Batman rather than the thugs he originally set out to impress. Most of Signalman's criminal exploits, then, were quickly halted when Batman decided to take a few seconds to kick him in the face.

Where to Find Them

Potential henchmen are everywhere. They're standing on the side of the road waiting for the landscaping truck to come pick them up. They're changing the oil in the fryer. They're toiling in America's prisons. They're standing in the nation's unemployment lines. They're coming back from wars all over the world and don't know what to do with themselves. They're gathering in huge numbers at comic book conventions. They're graduating from any number of liberal arts colleges.

If you're too lazy to do any active recruiting (and hey, who can blame you, since coming up with a pitch-perfect name like 'The Master Controller' takes a lot of work and time), there's an answer for you, too: A staffing firm. Specifically, one which the GBM Local 662 recommended to me as they simultaneously demonstrated how my car trunk door worked on my thumbs. Unions, man.

So, hey, be sure to contact Hench Head Hunters International today! Triple-H-I will find just the right henchmen for you, or kill trying! (Please hire from them, I beg of you.)

What you Should Call Them

When speaking to the group, it's okay to call your henchmen generic names like "henchmen," or "minions." In fact, it might help keep you from gaining any sort of emotional attachment to them, which would be a big mistake. Eventually, they are going to be obliterated into a fine powder. It's only a matter of time.

When addressing them individually, you could give them each a number or some kind of barcode or something, but that's a little generic.

Why not put a little personality into it, and provide them with some entertaining names that might also be fun to say? As long as it doesn't lead to your being depressed after their eventual slaughter, it's a good idea and keeps things around the lair interesting. Plus, if one of your whimsically named henchmen gets eaten alive or something, you can just name another one that same thing and forget about the whole ordeal with your loyal employee being digested slowly over a matter of decades.

Depending on how many you have on staff, you could even name your henchmen individually or as a full group.

I'll give you an example. Let's say your supervillain persona is something like "Mr. Insomnia." You use your powers to keep people from sleeping until lack of sleep makes them enter a trance-like state that allows you to control their every action with the slightest suggestion. Simple enough.

Now, let's also say that you have two henchmen on staff. Not nearly enough, but you're new to the game and you're still trying to prove yourself. You don't have enough cash on hand to pay anyone (or, you promise to pay them and then don't). Right now, all you can afford is the two. Okay, so what to call them? You're going to want to come up with some nicknames that go along with your villain theme. So, maybe "Toss" and "Turn?" Or "Caffeine" and "Sugar?" Or, better yet, "Traffic Noise" and "Barking Dog." Any of those would work splendidly.

Let's skip forward a few years. You've been quite successful, and your operations have grown substantially. You've got so many henchmen on staff now that it'll take way too much of your time to come up with individual names for each of them, and your henchmen can't come up with their own names for you. They can barely even remember to eat every day.

So, it's time to come up with a general name for the whole group. Some possibilities might be: "The Zzzzzs" (irony can work), "Bed Bugs," "The Night Terrors," "Blood-shots," "Severe Back Pains," "MMORPGs."

The main thing here is to be creative, and, for the love of crap, never think of them as people . . . or even pets. They are chattel. The only difference is they'll be chattel with a funny name.

Potential Henchmen: Everywhere You Look, Including Your Local Department Store

People have to deal with customers like this every day. Don't you think they'd get a lot more out of the wicked world of henching? We sure do.

* * *

"Listen up, Jared—is it Jared? You've . . . you've got a little ketchup on your nametag there. I think it might have dripped down from the stain in your half-grown crustache and onto your sternum while you scarfed down handfuls of greasy French fries all afternoon. Look, Jared, I've been standing in line here for about four hours now, so I'd prefer you pay attention. I bought this roll of Stik 'n' Stay masking tape here yesterday and, son, I'm just going to put it out there for you. This is some of the most embarrassing masking tape I've seen in my entire life.

"Frankly, my friend, I would be ashamed to sell this masking tape to even non-discerning and unintelligent customers. And then there are the people like me, who find your lack of quality masking tape simply insulting.

"Let me make this a little clearer for you, since you seem to be replaying the theme from 'The A-Team' over and over in your head as I tell you this. Actually, first, let me ask you, Jared, what would you consider to be the two main functions of a roll of masking tape? I'll answer that question for you, since you look like you may be slowly choking on a hunk of congealed chicken fat stuck in your throat. The two main functions of the product are *masking* and *taping*. Let me repeat that for you, since your ears are plainly filled with enough waxy buildup to make a life-sized replica of the Pieta: Masking and taping.

"I'll start with masking. Let's take a big slab of this tape here—like so—and affix it to my face, with some makeshift eye holes and a little mouth hole, and some big ears for flare . . . and . . . there we go. Now, tell me Jared, can you still make out my features? Is my face fully obscured or has the purchase of this only semi-opaque masking tape entirely ruined my budding career in lucha libre wrestling as a high-flying sensation named El Gringo Machismo?

"Let me tell you, the fans at Burro Grande Semi-Professional Wrestling did not appreciate being able to make out my highly defined cheekbones. It ruined the illusion, they said.

"That's pathetic, Jared. If I could make a decently identity-hiding mask and had passed that course in vigilantism I took at the community college, I would have broken in and knocked over the snack bar's soda fountains right there in front of you, you unwashed cretin. And I would have felt good about it. Imagine all that 7-Up right there, all over the floor. That would have been on *you*.

"Are you listening or is the buzzing in your brain so loud from the time you sat on the speakers at the Crüe concert that you have permanent nerve damage?

"Let's move on to the second aspect of this joke of a product: the taping. This one roll of masking tape has ruined no fewer than six VCRs, four voice recorders, two 9-millimeter projectors, some very expensive editing equipment, and a Doberman. And I barely got half an episode of *CSI: Miami* out of it.

"Jared! Hey! Pay attention! You can spend all the time you want picturing your sister naked at home, but not on the job, partner. This is my time, damn it.

"I also would like to point out that this little roll of masking tape's serviceability as an adhesive was not exactly of the highest standard, either. I placed this stuff —rolled up so that it's sticky on both sides—on no fewer than twenty-seven toilets all around the state, and only landed 'News of the Weird' stories in around four major newspapers. Four, Jared! How many grandmothers do I have to almost permanently attach to toilet seats before I start getting a little recognition in the mainstream media? And, as far as I knew from what I read, there was little to no scarring or need for skin grafting.

"I blame you, Jared, you middle school dropout. I blame you and this uncaring, shoddy, un-American, filthy, badly located, understocked, pusillanimous, stinkily clienteled discount department store you've got going here."

"Now give me my forty-nine cents back."

* * *

Does this sound like your life? Consider joining the Global Brotherhood of Minions today! *

---

*   This has been a paid advertisement from THE GLOBAL BROTHER-
    HOOD OF MINIONS

How to Dress Them

Just like you should name your henchmen in a way thematically similar to your supervillain identity, you should also dress them in costumes that are somehow related to your persona. Like, 'Surgeon Sinister' makes all his henchmen dress as demented candy stripers. Something like that.

The only thing you need to be keenly aware of is that it's imperative that you never let your henchmen dress in costumes cooler than yours. In fact, they should never do anything cooler than you.

They get jobs, you get to be cool. It's in our contract with the aforementioned union, whom, I can't stress enough, you really need to listen to. (Please.)

Training Exercise 4: Disciple Discipline

It's inevitable. Your henchmen are going to do something that's out of line. It's what they do. But how to deal with such incompetence? By showing them who's boss, that's how. Think about how you would respond to the following scenario (or, better [worse] yet, try it out for real):

You finally have your local superhero group, The Truth Squad, in your sights. After weeks of planning and strategizing, you order your army of loyal minions to attack their stronghold, the Veracity Venue. They pour out of your headquarters and into the field, fired up from your rousing, highly threatening pep talk. You sit back and relax, content that the operation can't possibly go wrong.

Your henchmen return several hours later than you expected, only to inform you that everything went wrong. They accidentally attacked the wrong building. And the building they did attack just happened to be your lawyer's house. So now she's not talking to you. And they wrecked your airship.

They shrug their shoulders and mumble "sorry" sbefore slinking off to their barracks to watch movies about people doing shit in spaceships.

* * *

If you said you would . . .

Threaten to quit, run into your bedroom and cry, you should probably then wait a few years before turning pro.

Revoke their telephone and TV privileges, you should maybe consider opening a day care and forgetting the whole supervillain thing.

Confine them to their quarters, you clearly lack an understanding of henchmen. That's their favorite place to be, where they can read comics and masturbate all day long.

Make them go try again, you're enacting a valid punishment, since henchmen hate work, but you're running the risk of having them screw up even worse and possibly blow up your own HQ.

Force them to all apologize to your attorney, you're not really teaching them proper evil values, and your lawyer's a bitch, anyway. She won't give a shit.

Kill one of them as an example to the others, that'll probably put some fear into them, and you get to kill someone. It's a double-whammy.

Scream at them for hours and hours, calling them worthless dog feces, you're not really treating them any differently than normal.

Wipe them all out in a fiery rain of death, you have admirable evil rage, but are going to have a pretty hard time finding new employees in the future.

Chapter 8

Facilities*

Note that the exterior of your volcano headquarters will never be fully visible to the non-helicopter-owning portion of the population.

---

* Chapter 8 is sponsored by CREEPY ATMOSPHERICS INC., "Putting the 'wooo' in your 'eeooooo.'"

Supervillainy is a business, and, as a business, you're going to need a base of operations. It's just that yours is going to be called a lair or a hideout instead of a central processing center or a manufacturing headquarters or whatever corporate types are calling their shit these days.

Much like any up-and-coming business, you're going to need to find a place that can suit all your needs. You know, like:

Restaurants need big kitchens where waiters and cooks can conveniently spit and urinate in your food.

Advertising agencies need big conference rooms where the employees can come up with new ways to lie to people.

Banks need big vaults that executives can snort cocaine off of and have sex on top of your money while they simultaneously fritter it away.

(It couldn't hurt to model yourself after those guys.) Here are some things you should keep in mind when you're looking for some office space for your supervillain upstart.

Bare Essentials

A Command Center

This is where you execute your plans (and if you so wish, many people). Amenities should most likely include a prominent, throne-like chair from which you can shout commands; a giant viewing-screen; communications equipment; seating for henchmen as they push buttons and turn knobs; lots of buttons and knobs; blinking lights; large staircases that probably go nowhere; trap doors; your logo on everything.

A War Room

A conference room where you and your chief lieutenants can plot out your devilishly evil, well thought out plan. It likely needs a large, round table; mood lighting; lots of ornately fashioned chairs; giant maps on the walls.

Escape Pods

You will use these. Often.

Restrooms

For you. Not necessarily for the henchmen.

An Armory

You never know when you're going to need some dart guns, jet packs, or laser cannons. But, in general, you will need them all the time.

A Parking Garage

To protect your high-speed killing machines from the elements and/or possible rival villains who have an affinity for stealing your awesome, hopefully flying, cars.

A Kitchen

For when you need emergency Doritos. Which will be often.

A Brig or Dungeon

You have to keep your prisoners somewhere, and unfortunately, because they harbor information, you can't kill them all. But hey, you don't have to make it nice or anything.

Good (Bad) to Have

Henchmen's Quarters

It's a smart idea to keep them on campus in case of a midnight superhero attack or if the pipes burst or something. You can make their quarters basically the same as the brig, just so they don't get complacent.

Your Quarters

In case you feel the need to stay on-hand at all times. On the one hand, you'll be there to keep things in order if the shit hits the fan. On the other hand, you might get trapped inside your fiery tomb when the aforementioned shit hits the aforementioned fan. Up to you here.

A Throne Room

Separate from the Command Center, this would be where your mask is mechanically affixed to your face, you can talk to yourself at length, and you can call henchmen in to stand before you to be berated. It's a good idea to have some trap doors in here, too.

A Library

Where you could store thousands upon thousands of copies of this book.

Large Storage Rooms

Because you've got to keep your various death traps and doomsday devices somewhere.

Huge Aquariums

Because you've got to keep your gigantic mutated piranhas somewhere.

A Morgue

Because you have to keep the corpses of your victims and various henchmen somewhere.

SUPERVILLAIN HISTORY FACT

The 1972 Washington Redskins, a team comprised entirely of supervillains, made a valiant effort that year to defeat the Miami Dolphins, an undefeated team of superheroes who had infiltrated the NFL. In that year's Super Bowl, the Redskins successfully transported Los Angeles Memorial Coliseum to hell, where they planned to abandon the Dolphins and all the fans in attendance. Unfortunately, Dolphins kicker Garo Yepremian botched a field goal which was supposed to seal the portal to hell and allow the villains to escape. The stadium returned to Los Angeles, and the Dolphins lived to hero another day.

Completely Unnecessary, But Cool

A Hallway Filled With Lasers that Can Cut Intruders to Pieces

Like in the *Resident Evil* movie. It's the only thing you remember from that movie, sure, but it was super badass.

A Shrine To Your Superhero Nemesis

To really solidify the whole creepy obsession, "hate is a passion, too," vibe.

Trampoline Room

A trampoline room would be sweet.

A Laboratory With a Full Working Staff, Creating All-New, All-Evil Gadgets Like a Drink that Looks and Tastes Like Orange Juice, but Is Actually Toxic Waste

Or a wristwatch that contains a tiny homicidal man.

Or a ballpoint pen with which you can stain and ruin superhero costumes.

It'll be like James Bond, but, you know, villainous.

A Coffee Shop

To give off to passers-by the appearance of being a legitimate business. Plus, free coffee.

A Colosseum-Style Arena

Because you're almost certainly going to need to have a couple superheroes fight to the death at some point. And hey, on a slow day, why not throw a couple henchmen in there!

With a tiger!!

And some acid!!!

A Pool Room

Where you can fill your swimming pool with pool tables while betting on a dead pool.

Avoid

An Employee Lounge

The last thing you're going to want your henchmen doing is lounging. Contrary to popular belief, idle hands aren't the devil's playthings.

A Cave

Too superhero-y, by far.

A Bar

If you're going to drink, especially with your henchmen, you need to do it elsewhere . . . preferably where other people can clean up puke, blood, and henchman limbs so you don't have to.

A Room Where Reality Is Warped Beyond Recognition, Like an M.C. Escher Painting, Where Down Is Up, Up Is Down, the Walls Stretch To Infinity and To Stare Too Far Into the Distance Is To Peer Into the Face of Madness

Neat if you're trying to drive a superhero insane, but a serious bitch when it's three in the morning and you're just trying to get to the kitchen for a late-night grilled cheese.

A Secret Access Tunnel

Cool as hell, but to include it is akin to asking your rivals to find it, enter your stronghold, and take over. And you don't need that.

Stasis Tubes for Your Various Clones

Clones are always a bad idea.

First, because they give you a window into just how obnoxious and insufferable you are.

Second, because they're constantly melting.

A Tribunal Chamber/Courtroom

It might seem like a good idea to include a room where you can hold trials/examinations/crucibles, but you have to keep in mind that irony is always lurking around the corner, waiting to bite you in the ass. And irony loves it when you're convicted and sentenced to execution in your own court-room. Bet on that.

A Hall of Justice

I don't even know why you would consider having this.

PROFILES IN LAME SUPERVILLAINY

Asbestos Man

History: Chemist Orson Kasloff became a criminal after years of being a respected scientist failed to pay off the way he expected. He envied his fellow scientists, who he often saw riding around in Maseratis and banging super-models, like, every night, because that's obviously what scientists do all the time. He didn't get much respect as a criminal, though, and decided the best way to quickly gain a rep would be to defeat the Human Torch. So he challenged him to a fight in a letter and created an asbestos costume.

M.O.: The Asbestos Man created a flame-retardant asbestos suit to fight the Torch and used a fancy net to rope him in. The Torch rendered him instantly useless when he broke Asbestos Man's net. Then he laughed at him for wearing a suit that would cause him to inhale particles of a known carcinogen.

Location, Location, Location: Some Common Hideouts and How They May (Or May Not) Work For You

Abandoned Warehouse

Pros: Inconspicuous and unlikely to be mistaken for an occupied warehouse, especially if you take time to break out all the windows; lots of floor space; usually located near docks, and we supervillains and other criminals are always doing shit at the docks.

Cons: Not particularly luxurious; highly cliché, and therefore the first place superheroes are likely to look; sure to cause some awkwardness once some developer tries to rezone and make it into condos.

Skyscraper

Pros: Makes you feel awesome as you stand in your office and look down on the city you will soon crush; provides a great place for you to stare down your superhero rival as he or she floats outside; the appearance of legitimacy.

Cons: Downtown property is extremely expensive; you might have to actually run a successful business; having to keep up the appearance of legitimacy.

Underwater Fortress

Pros: Hard for the police to get to; constant cool stuff going on behind you; the inevitability of a really cool sequence where you have to make it surface.

Cons: One crack and you're totally screwed, and superheroes will crack it, because they care about other people's property not one bit; also, whale sex is disgusting.

Cavernous Underground Bunker

Pros: Space galore, and it's easy to expand if you need to; transportation through cool tubes and tunnels; the giant ants can really be of use if you can control them.

Cons: It's what we at the ISS have, so to get one would really be biting our style; hard to light; very hot; the giant ants can really be a hindrance if you don't know how to control them.

Military Base

Pros: Spread out over a large area so you're harder to target; lots of vehicles on-hand; a good (bad) environment for yelling.

Cons: Early mornings; constant walking despite the presences of numerous vehicles; the possibility of being mistaken for a real U.S. Army base and being closed due to budget cuts.

Abandoned Amusement Park/Circus

Pros: Very, very creepy; old rides provide the perfect venue for unnecessary chases; cages galore.

Cons: Rickety old crap is sure to break, and superheroes have all the luck; henchmen are easily freaked out by clowns; cages galore.

Remote Observatory

Pros: Those giant telescopes look awesome and can easily be replaced with a cannon designed to destroy the moon; wear a lab coat and you won't even look out-of-place; no one ever goes to the observatory anymore.

Cons: Not a whole lot of space outside of the telescope room; hard to get to; the people who do come to the observatory . . . ugh.

Inside a Volcano

Pros: Easy to carve the shape of your face into the side; intimidating, especially if the volcano is still active; inconspicuous (unless you do the whole face-carving thing).

Cons: Construction is very difficult and costly; volcanoes are rarely found in major cities, thus making your commute pretty lengthy; you could lose your whole operation in one earth-burp.

Your Own Island

Pros: Nice weather; lots and lots of space; no federal authorities to muck up your plans.

Cons: No local population to torment; sand gets in everything; nice weather.

Inside a Major Landmark or Monument

Pros: Nothing says "I mean business" more than seizing the Eiffel Tower or Mount Rushmore; very picturesque; most are centrally located.

Cons: Federal authorities are real assholes when it comes to their monuments; most don't include any of the advanced computer equipment you need; tourists.

Deep In a Large Canyon

Pros: Many of the benefits of an underground headquarters, but with much less digging; river access; possible hidden alien technology.

Cons: Donkey riding is really tedious; cave-ins are pretty much a given; possible hidden alien technology that could make you into a quivering ball of gelatin.

Clock Tower

Pros: Well-situated in a major city; gears and shit make for great fight staging; dramatic clanging during your climactic battles.

Cons: Dramatic clanging at any other time is incredibly obnoxious; gears really hurt; the whole hero hanging off the clock hands thing is totally played.

An Ornate Building or Castle with Gothic Architecture

Pros: Really makes a statement of your villainous power; pretty much the perfect thematic match for a super-villain; moats.

Cons: Not terribly inconspicuous; drafty; difficult to repair after a superhero comes crashing through your hand-carved stone walls.

Earth-Orbiting Satellite

Pros: Damn near unreachable for superheroes who need oxygen and have no access to spaceships; looks super-cool; the Space Police barely pay attention to this sector.

Cons: Damn near unreachable for you if you need oxygen and have no access to spaceships; gravity issues; re-entry really sucks.

On the Moon

Pros: Again with the oxygen/spaceships; great for when your plans have to do with global destruction, because it provides safety and such a great view; instant weight loss.

Cons: Again with the oxygen/spaceships (again); other villains who always want to blow up the moon; the need for caution, because if the moon hits your eye like a big pizza pie, that's amore.

In a Pocket Universe

Pros: Pretty much infinite space; locals who are often easily made into henchmen armies; cheap and/or free building materials.

Cons: Possibly too much space, and therefore very easy to get lost; locals who can pretty easily turn on you; portals are fickle little things, and strand you with impunity.

Hell

Pros: You're going to end up there anyway, so it's good to get a head start; very difficult access, especially for superheroes; lots of possible like-minded collaborators on-hand.

Cons: Difficult to leave once you complete your plans; the heat; the sodomy can really break your concentration.

Your Mom's Basement

Pros: Cheap rent; a layout you're already plenty familiar with; free spaghetti.

Cons: The washer and dryer make a lot of unwanted noise; constant nagging to do chores; a constant reminder that daddy will never come home.

Chapter 9

Planning[*]

Decoys are always useful.

---

* Chapter 9 is sponsored by SUPERVILLAIN ENERGY BAR COMPANY, "Regular energy bars, but these are for supervillains."

The Psychomonitor is about to explode with all the readers out there asking this mental question: "Okay, I've established my base of operations, put together my persona, set my goals, and gotten my qualifications in order. When do I get to go out there and mess some people up?"

Once you plan something, Mr. I-ask-really-obvious-questions-of-an-inanimate-book man.

We supervillains can't go flying half-cocked into any situation and just start smashing stuff. That's the superhero's game. They're reactive. But we're proactive, you see. We go out there and make things happen. And we do it with forethought.

Here are some tips to keep in mind when you're plotting your evil master plan:

Creativity is key

It's fine for you to pull out one of the old classics, like, say, poisoning the city's water supply. But you have to find new and innovative ways of doing it. Like, what if you figured out a way to change human biology so that water is poisonous to people? Except, don't do that one. I thought of that one. It's mine.

Make it understandable

We're talking henchmen-level understandable here. So be sure to include lots of pictures and few words of more than two syllables.

Go for grandiosity

Sliding in and near-invisibly robbing a bank is effective and all, but doing it while also causing big explosions or faking an alien invasion is more theatrical, and remember what we talked about in Chapter 1: You've got to stoke that flair for the dramatic.

Keep it in the family

It's extraordinarily bad form to go after another supervillain's nemesis. The only instances in which such a move is allowed are: If they attack you first, in the event of a villain feud or bet, superhero disguise switching, and team villainy.

Stick with your theme

If you're Killbeard the Pirate, a far-reaching political espionage plot isn't for you. Now, a plan to take over the White House and make it into a ship with which you'll go conquer Mars, home of your lifelong rival Deathbeard, that's more like it.

Don't aim too high or too low

Keep it street-level if that's your speed. If your powers are more cosmic, be sure to think big. A petty thief who attempts to accelerate the entropy in the universe is pretty misguided, as would be a galactic entity that can alter the fiber of space and time trying to crack a safe.

Make sure you have an out

Any plan that ends up with you perched on top of a cliff with no escape helicopter or some kind of rocket system that will propel the cliff and you with it to the next state over isn't a plan you want to have. Trust me on this one.

Avoid doing things you might regret later

Guilt is the supervillain's greatest enemy. You know, after superheroes. So if killing a convent full of nuns is going to make your nights uniformly sleepless, lay off, and consider stomping on some kittens instead.

With those things in mind, you're almost ready to meticulously construct your magnum opus. The only remaining step for you to take now is to figure out just what type of plan best fits your v-style. (That's insider evil slang for "villain style." We're way cool, you guys.) You've got a wide array of ways to go about your treacherous business, but some we might suggest are:

The direct approach

Go in, do your biz, get out. This is a great way to do things for villains who have luxuries like diplomatic immunity or god-like cosmic powers. For those who don't have those things, it's a really effective way of thrusting yourself (sometimes literally) into the public eye, but you should also be aware that it's going to result in your face getting smashed in the public eye as well.

Subterfuge

Whether it be a disguise, an invisibility cloak, a device that convinces everyone you encounter that you're actually their dad, or nothing more than a lot of sneaking around in corridors and ventilation systems, concealing your identity and your nefarious intentions can get you a long way toward accomplishing your goals without having to worry about superheroes or other interference. The downside here, of course, is that once you do turn UN Headquarters into a giant barbecue grill on which you will soon roast the world's leaders until they hand authority of their nations over to you, no one will know you were behind it. And notoriety is almost as important to the supervillain as success.

The wool-over-the-eyes routine

You know what's fun? Getting a superhero to do all the work for you! Seriously, all you have to do is tell them that some kids are gonna die or a nuclear power plant is melting down, and that they have to do such-and-such to stop it, and they'll totally do it! So you won't even have to dirty your hands getting your giant robot armor out of storage and re-activated. Of course, the big setback here is having to deal with the hero once they find out he or she got duped. They're terrible sports.

Creating a distraction

The plan from Training Exercise 1 is a good example. Use some kind of a distraction (another villain, a decoy of yourself, giant monkeys) to lure heroes and other authorities to a location far away from where you're going to be doing your actual work. Then, sneak in and do your evil deeds. Of course, just like with subterfuge, you get the gold but not the glory.

The false hope gambit

This is a great method for first-time villains who are otherwise unknown. Use political rhetoric to get in the public's good graces or work your way into a superhero team. Gain their trust. Set the trap. Then, when the time is right, bam! Snap down on them faster than Dr. Beartrap's jaws on Major Ursa. Of course, well-known villains won't be able to sneak this kind of stuff through, so they'll have to find some kind of puppet to send in. But that often works pretty well, too. This type of plan requires a lot of patience, though, and having to hang around with so-called "good" people for a large portion of your time. So be prepared for that. Try to find ways to comfort yourself, possibly compulsive masturbation or perhaps a new drug habit.

The for-its-own-sake approach

Anyone who's seen *Superman Returns*, and has thought about it for like, ten minutes, knows that Lex Luthor's plan to ruin the planet so he can sell the remaining inhabitable land for exorbitant rates is utterly ridiculous. What good is money on a ruined planet where there'll barely be anyone to buy stuff from, right? But obviously none of that really matters. All Lex was doing, and all you'll be doing if you choose this plan, is using the pretense of profit to engage in wanton worldwide destruction. And there ain't nothing wrong (or, I guess, right) with that. You should note, though, that people, especially comic fans, will constantly point out how stupid your plans were. Like, all the time. Some will mention it every day for the remainder of their pitiable lives. So it's probably better not to Google your name.

The way-too-complicated-to-even-make-sense approach

This type of plan is actually composed of several, if not dozens, of smaller plans. It may involve variations on every type of plan already mentioned, plus quite possibly several others even we have never thought of. The only real requirement here is that the whole thing be very, very long and almost obnoxiously over-thought. The best thing about these, as if I even have to really mention this, is that it runs superheroes plain old ragged to the point where, once they have ascended your meticulously constructed tower to the heavens, which is designed to harness the ionic energy in the air to power your device designed to reverse the earth's polarity, thereby allowing you to open a luxury resort in the Yukon Territory (or maybe cause the ice caps to melt and put lots of the world's major city's underwater, however you want to go with it), they'll be so tired and worn out that all you'll have to do is thump them and they'll tumble over like a bag full of rocks. Now, you should be aware that it's going to be pretty exhausting for you, too. Getting the child you kidnapped from an orphanage and brainwashed to be the perfect politician elected president and then triggering him or her to declare war on all superheroes is downright exhausting, even if you're keeping your distance and managing the whole thing from a secluded bunker filled with TV screens. I mean, lots and lots of things have to go right for these plans, which can take months, if not years, to go just the way you want them to. And there are lots of people out there who can't stand to see us actually accomplish anything.

All I'm saying is, get your fist ready, cause you're probably going to need to shake it!

SUPERVILLAIN HISTORY FACT

Despite the many nicknames which would seem to indicate otherwise, Microsoft CEO Bill Gates has never been a supervillain. Gates is merely a robot puppet created by the A.I. known as MICROSOFT, which is actually a sentient, evil being which aims to infect every computer and person in the world with a virus within the next twenty-five years.

The Other Type of Planning: Financial

While you may think you exist completely outside the bounds of regular society (and yes, we do tend to laugh malevolently at most cultures' so-called "rules" and hardly ever pick up after our dogs), like it or not, you're going to need money.

Yes, it's easy enough to steal a death ray or a teleportation machine if it's on a train from London to New York (of course, this would happen in the future, after they develop ocean trains), but what if you have to build your super-weapon yourself? Sure, you could steal all the parts and put it together on your own, but that shit's hard.

So whatever your situation—buying the finished death ray, buying the parts or hiring people to put it together for you; face it, kid, you gotta have that cheese. (That's street lingo for money. You'll recall from earlier that we are incredibly hip.)

How To Get It

Probably the most obvious way, and the path most villains take is to steal it. And that's fine. If that's what works best for you, go with that.

But theft isn't everybody's thing, and that's okay, too. There are plenty of other ways to get the cash you're going to need to pay your henchmen (or to at least give off the illusion that you plan to pay them) and any of the various hookers you may hire over the course of a given night of supervillainous loose morals.

Extortion/black mail

Profitable and fun! Plenty of your supervillain colleagues (and, for that matter, lots of superheroes and cops) have lots of things they wouldn't want getting out to their significant others or kids or parish priests (or the police.). For instance, Muy Caliente, the Fire-Breathing Luchadore, likes to have "wrestling matches" with goats every other weekend. Obviously, I can't use that particular bit of damning information anymore, because I just revealed it to everyone reading this, but it doesn't matter. There are plenty of other secrets I'm holding onto.[*]

Counterfeiting

All you really need for this one is a good printer, some source material (the plates they use to print bills are pretty easy to come by, as long as you have someone working for you in the government, and we pretty much all do), and some very, very gullible heavy artillery salespeople.

Black market sales

You'd be surprised how much someone is willing to pay for a baby carrying a balloon full of heroin inside an illegal assault weapon.

Pyramid and/or Ponzi schemes

People are totally willing to give you virtually all their money, as long as you tell them they'll make a return. Even if you have no proof whatsoever that they will. It's beautiful.

---

[*] It's a good idea to keep some cash on hand at all times, because there's going to be lots of stuff you do that you don't want your lady and/or fella to find out, either, and pretty much everyone you know is going to try to use it against you.

Merchandising

People will pay through the nose for a badly sculpted plastic doo-dad or some low-quality bed sheets as long as it has a picture of someone who vaguely looks like a character from a movie on it . . . especially if it's mint-in-box. So be sure to put everything in boxes.

Evil Dentistry

There are a lot of gold fillings out there in the world. All you need is a diploma and a license, and they can be yours.

Legitimate business

Works great for when you're in court, since you get to use the old "Your honor, I'm just a simple, hard-working entrepreneur" routine on the judge. That'll always get you out of a lot of jams. Of course, the real problem with legitimate business is the whole work aspect of it, along with hiring employees and obeying labor laws and all that junk. It's really a lot of trouble. But hey, there are some benefits.

Advertiser support

Corporations don't care who it is putting their name out there, as long as more kids eat their overly sweet breakfast cereals.

Magically creating money out of thin air

It requires a very specific skill-set (one that In-Genie-ous happens to have), but boy, is it useful. Look into it.

PROFILES IN LAME SUPERVILLAINY

Hypno-Hustler

History: A mysterious fellow known only as Antoine became the Hypno-Hustler and began stealing valuables from club owners and audiences when he played shows with his band, the Mercy Killers. Presumably he did so because he knew disco was on its way out, and he wanted to make sure he had a nice nest egg for the following years, when he would probably be working at the Gap.

M.O.: The Hypno-Hustler used a pair of special hypnotic goggles to mesmerize club owners and audiences on the nights of his shows and force them to hand over all their money and jewelry to him. Unfortunately for him, Spider-Man discovered the secret to foiling all his well-laid plans: covering his ears.

Managing Your Money

You may have a relatively steady income through various illegal means, but that doesn't mean you should start burning through it like Ignatius Ignition through a billboard. You never know when that flow's going to shut off when you suddenly get thrown into a federal ultra-maximum security super-prison for no good reason. And you're not going to want to have to come back and rebuild your whole operation from scratch. So here are some tips for keeping or even growing your nest egg.

Spend wisely

In fact, don't spend when you don't have to. For instance, you can offer to pay that assassin to kill your nemesis, but kill him or her afterward. Or you could hire an engineer to build your underwater headquarters for you, and when it comes time to pay him, you kill him or her. Or say you employ someone to handle your finances for you, but as soon as he or she asks for any of that money they've been handling, kill him or her. In fact, the only circumstance in which you should actually pay anyone is if they are immortal or if you could somehow need them for something in the future. But we can't think of any reasons why you would.

Make good investments

An example of a good investment would be a teleportation device that you could use to transport all of the gold they keep in Fort Knox (or wherever they keep in now) to your personal vault.

Keep it laundered

Tie it up in things like candy, ice cream, and garbage collection companies. You know, things that could never be associated with criminal activity.

Don't spend extravagantly

Do you really need the XT-9000 model Natchez brand death ray when you get the XT-8500 for nearly $40,000 less? Couldn't you live with the smaller death ray? It's cheaper, it will kill a whole lot of people, too, and you'll maintain your sizable bank account. (Though, we do have to say, the XT-9000 is really great. Oh, you know what's better, though? The XR-99666. Man, that thing is sweet. We probably wouldn't settle for less.)

Chapter 10

Limitations*

This will happen often. Invest in nose splints.

---

* Chapter 10 is sponsored by CONSOLIDATED RESURRECTORS, "Guaran-
teed to bring you back with all your limbs intact or your giant laser-hook is
free!"

So, you're now excited beyond all belief to jump right into the bustling world of supervillainy. You've got plans for a headquarters all drawn up. You've come up with a logo for yourself and a catchphrase and everything. You're ready to go. I know that because the Psychomonitor is blinking and flashing and even smoking a little right now. But don't get it twisted, blinking, flashing, smoking readers: There's some stuff in this game you ain't gonna like.

Look, I'm not going to sugarcoat this for you. When you go into villainy, you will get punched in the face. Like, every day. Sometimes, you'll just be walking to the corner store for some Moon Pies and Fanta, and then BAM! All of a sudden your jaw is vertical.

Now, upon that revelation, I see that the Psychomonitor has calmed down considerably. I can also see that many of you are more or less infuriated that I waited until the last chapter of the book to make this clear. "I had to muddle through nine chapters' worth of your blabbering about superpowers and costume types and death rays, and now you tell me this?" is the specific question many of you are thinking.

Allow me to remind you at this point, if you didn't notice or have somehow forgotten, that I am a professional supervillain. If I didn't do something at least a little bit evil in the process of me writing and you reading this book, I wouldn't be doing my job. Learn from my example, folks. Learn from me.

And unfortunately for you, I'm not done yet doing my evil deed of informing you of some of the downsides of professional supervillainy. While punching is almost certainly the liability you're going to have to deal with most often, and probably the most physically painful of the bunch, there are lots of other things you're going to want to be aware of, too. Here's some of the biggest:

Incarceration

I'm sad to say that one thing that tends to happen after a face-punching incident is that you will often be taken to local, federal, or worldwide authorities and put into some kind of jail. If you're lucky, say, your costume is ridiculous enough or you laugh at inappropriate times or you keep talking to an invisible, floating man who keeps playing tricks on you and everyone around you, you may instead get trundled off to a home for the criminally insane or, in the best-case scenario, get no punishment other than to be ordered into some kind of rehab-style treatment program (thanks, Democrats).

Luckily, it's pretty easy to break out of just about any of these various prisons, even the ones where they cryogenically freeze you and shoot you into space. I mean, come on, superheroes need us as much as we need them, if not more, and their fans don't want new, badly-thought-out characters filling up their comic pages. They want their straight-up nemeses in there, getting punched in the face for their enjoyment. So the heroes' associations make sure the guards look the other way, we break out, and the cycle continues.

Dealing with henchmen

I talked about this quite a bit in Chapter 7, if you'll recall, but to reiterate: They smell bad; they're very stupid; they're probably going to screw things up; they eat all your food; and they smell really, really bad.

Public hatred

The average shlub doesn't get that balance is necessary for the universe, and that for every good, there must also be an evil. The regular Joe out there in the world just isn't very Zen, you know? They're not going to understand you. Especially considering all the anti-villain bile that's out there in the popular media. Comic books, movies, TV shows, every book except for this one, and about everything else out there in the zeitgeist is against us. Be aware, then, that you'll never be popular, and, odds are, you're going to get spit on when all you're trying to do is go out to the Redbox to rent *Seven*, every villain's favorite feel-good (bad) film.

SUPERVILLAIN HISTORY FACT

The entire nation of Belgium is, in fact, a supervillain. We don't mean its people when we say that. We mean the actual land itself is a supervillain. That's because, in 1985, the superhero then known as Captain Vacuum spread the Dirt Dervish all over the country after sucking him up into his super-powerful giant vacuum cleaner. Now, Dirt Dervish has seeped into the land of all of Belgium and resides there, as the country itself. That's why Belgium occasionally shoves France, or creates really bad smells that seep into the Netherlands.

Rivalries with other villains

These can actually be a lot of fun sometimes, but they can also sometimes lead to sabotaged headquarters, dead henchmen, and stolen significant others. We supervillains are a territorial bunch, and if we feel like we're threatened, or we just kind of feel like threatening you, watch out. No, really, literally watch out . . . because we're coming after you with our car; or maybe one of our Terrordactyls.

General bad luck

Get ready to have your equipment fail, for accidents in which a gun goes off during a struggle to never go your way, for your minions to betray you, for security cameras to always pick you up and for serendipity to otherwise never smile upon you. Or let's just say, for example, that you're a reptilian bad guy who lives in a castle for some reason and has a thing for kidnapping princesses. Your ethnic stereotype plumber nemesis will always, *always* find the conveniently placed axe behind you, which he will then use to chop down the badly engineered bridge on which you always stand. Why? Because writers or God or whoever's in charge of plotting out the goings-on of the world simply have some kind of axe to grind against those in the business of evil. They're totally biased and it's totally unfair. But we have to be up to the challenge. We'll show them one of these days that the bad in the world deserves a fair shake.

Frequent deaths and rebirths

The good news is: If you're popular enough, you can pretty much never die. You can be in all kinds of situations in which it totally looks like you should be dead, like, maybe you go down with an exploding blimp or you eat a bomb and it blows up inside you or your entire body gets enveloped by spider-snakes (that's a snake with eight legs). But you'll come back a few months later, no worse for wear, just like you'll always get out of prison.

The trouble here is that, well, you do actually kind of have to die. Yeah, you may get your thought patterns placed inside a robot body. Or maybe you can transfer your brain to a clone of your arch-nemesis (always a nice touch). Or, if you're really good (bad), you'll up and get better for no good reason. But that blimp's gonna blow up. And that bomb's going to tear up your insides. And those spider-snakes are going to ensnare you in their webs, toy with you for several days, and then ingest you in one big bite. It's gonna happen. And that shit's gonna hurt.

Kite-Man

History: Charles Brown was a two-bit hood who devised a way to escape from the sites of his many petty thefts: by flying away on a kite strapped to his back. It should be noted that he thought this idea to be better than possibly flying a small plane or developing some rocket boots or figuring out a way to move really fast underground. Nope. A kite was his first choice.

M.O.: In addition to flying away on a kite, a terrific way to attract the attention of Batman, Superman and Hawkman, by the way, Kite-Man really stuck to the gimmick by attacking his enemies with small kites. Imagine the horror of having a barrage of kites hurled at you. "The sticks . . . if they hit you just right . . . are kind of pokey! Aaaaaaaaaggh!"

If you feel like you can handle all these setbacks—and we implore you not to forget the whole punching-in-the-face aspect of all this—then you, dear reader, are all set to enter the villainous arts.

If these issues seem like too much for you to deal with, well, it might be time to look into other lines of work. Maybe being a circus clown? You get to wear the same type of ridiculous (um . . . we mean, awesome) costume as we villains do and you still get the opportunity to be creepy as hell. Or why not start a private military company, like Blackwater? You'll get to blow plenty of shit up that way and, bonus, you'll never be held accountable.

Or you could finally write that novel you've wanted to get cracking on for so long. Here's a plot-starter for you: The president of the new one-world government holds Earth's last rainforest hostage, and only one man, an ex-black-ops specialist who now lives in a secluded cabin in northern Greenland, can recover the cure for cancer, which, incidentally, is in the rainforest.

That's free, readers.

Training Exercise 5: Bringing On, Working Through, or Going Around the Pain

For this exercise, you're going to need to do something big and public. Like, let's say, threaten to shoot a rocket at the mayor's motorcade. That should work. So, threaten to fire a rocket at the mayor's motorcade, and as you make public your threat, probably best done via a TV station you've overtaken, make sure it's pretty clear where you're broadcasting from and that the local superhero(es) have lots of clues to figure out where you are (they need all the help they can get). Then, just sit back and wait for them to arrive. Read a magazine. Twiddle your thumbs. Do whatever you need to kill time before the superhero or superhero team gets there.

When they finally do get to your broadcast location and bellow out some silly battle cry, you . . .

A) . . . respond with your own battle cry and jump right into the fray, loaded for bear . . . with your fists!
B) . . . pull out your particle cannon and start blasting away.
C) . . . send waves of henchmen after them. Once they are laid out, send hundreds more.
D) . . . immediately use your arm-mounted tele-portation device to quickly escape to a Crispy Cream.

E) . . . try to negotiate a truce with the heroes.

F) . . . drop to your knees and whimper. When they turn their backs in disgust, hit them with a folding chair.

G) . . . throw your hands in the air and go with them willingly before anyone gets hurt.

H) . . . drop onto the ground, assume the fetal position and cry until they feel sorry for you and leave.

If you chose option . . .

A) Your gung-ho attitude is admirable, but you may want to look this hyphenate up: "self-preservation." Also, you're probably very obnoxious at parties.

B) You're doing a good job of keeping your distance from the fight, but you're also risking irreparable damage to all your expensive and cool stuff, which, by the way, you should have with you at all times.

C) A very worthwhile option. It keeps you out of the brouhaha, takes the fight to the heroes and is really the best of all possible uses for henchmen. The only problem with this option is that you will eventually run out of henchmen, and will have to sneak out of a back door at some point.

D) It's fine to be a coward, but you'd be better served if you at least gave the slightest appearance of bravery, even if that means taking at least one punch before teleporting out of town.

Also, you may want to watch the diet, chunky. Try teleporting to Whole Foods or something.

E) Heroes never keep truces. And you'd probably never even manage to get a word out, anyway. If heroes have their heart set on punching, they're gonna do some punching.

F) The old Ric Flair maneuver. Sure, it makes you look like a sniveling, heartless coward, but you get to hit some people with a folding chair, so it basically evens out.

G) Lame. At least try to give 'em a little kick in the shins or something, guys.

H) Shameful, certainly. But you get to live to fight another day, and it sets some really low expectations for your next scheme. Prove them wrong, supervillain! Prove them wrong!

Conclusion

And so ends *The Supervillain Handbook*.

Do you feel prepared for the fast-paced world of villainy? Have you been thinking very hard about it? Think harder, readers. Think about your full lives. Re-think every idea and conception that has ever crept into your shallow brains.

And now, dear readers, we wish to thank you. Because we have now stolen all of your thoughts.

The Psychomonitor is no mere measurement device, gullible book-buyer (or borrower, or thief). It is a thought collector. And now that those thoughts are ours, we plan to use them against all of you.

Yes, that's right, fools! A worldwide blackmail scheme designed to bring you all to your knees! We know about that time you accidentally crapped the bed and that time you intentionally crapped the bed!

Prepare for the new-world revolution, peons! You will now bow to us and only us! Give up your lazy, unoriginal dreams of supervillainy! Did you dare to think we would allow you to enter the profession we have striven for so long to control without opposition?

Serve solely as our minions, answering to our every beck and call, bowing to our every whim, jumping before we even have to say it. You have no choice but to obey.

Your thoughts are now ours.[*]

---

[*]   This time, I really got you (and your thoughts), didn't I?

The ISS Timeline

1907

The Western Association of Ruffians is founded by Heinrich Misan-throach, William Howard Taft and others whose names are lost to history (the Association's record keepers were a vindictive bunch). Its founders succeed in replacing Theodore Roosevelt with a robotic version of himself.

1912

Unfortunately, robot Roosevelt is cursed with faulty memory circuits. After a lengthy battle with its original founders, he briefly takes over the Association and re-names it "The Bull Moose Party."

1916-1918

Association members fight on both sides of the Great War, not because of any ideological ties to the parties involved, but with the express intention of prolonging the war until the creation of the Ultimate Mustard Gas.

1921

Disappointed with the mustard gases created during World War I, the Association develops a gas that combines all condiments into a cornu-copia of deadly death. They are disappointed to find that the mayonnaise matrix is incorrectly calibrated, and it only kills about halfway.

1925

Mr. Wonderful and a group of other heroes gather to form the League of Right Rightness. At their first induction ceremony, the League battles the Association in a month-long fight in the middle of Vatican City. The fight doesn't end until the Illuminati show up and yell that they're trying to get some sleep.

1928

A short "supervillain craze" hits Europe. At the Amsterdam Summer Olympics, athletes compete in Laser-Ray Shooting at live human targets in the first and last villain-based Olympic event.

1929

The Association stages a stock-market "crash" in October in a plan to get the business-minded League to jump out of tall buildings. They all did, but then they flew away. It wasn't the smartest plan. The faked crash has some minor economic implications over the following decade.

1932

Franklin Delano Roosevelt, cousin of the Theodore Roosevelt robot, is elected president of the United States. FDR, a supervillain by trade, often has to hide from the public that his robot cousin had used his Polio Ray on him when he was a child.

1933

FDR creates the first "New Deal," an economic plan based on the ruse of the 1929 stock market crash. FDR's intent was to funnel all of the world's remaining money into the government, then steal it. But the plan backfired and the economy began a decade-long recovery.

1939

Adolf Hitler becomes the largest employer of supervillains in history after supervillains FDR and Mussolini lobby him to invade Poland, just to see what happens.

1945

The end of World War II leads to long negotiations regarding how the world should be divided up amongst the Association, the League and the normals. In the midst of the fist fighting, the Association breaks up into two factions: The Western Association of Ruffians and the Worldwide Conglomeration of Super-Criminals, who don't matter and we won't ever mention again.

1952

Dwight D. Eisenhower, the first superhero American president, is elected to office. The Association enters a period of decline in which members' largest accomplishments are the occasional malt shop robbery.

1961

Following a very slow decade, two enterprising young supervillains (one of whom is both a doctor and a king, ahem) seize control of the Association and rename it The International Society of Supervillains. A new era of villainy begins.

1963

After months and months of planning, the ISS carries out its first major plan: To use its Freak-Out Ray to turn most of the United States' upstanding teens and kids into sweaty, dirty hippies. The plan is a huge success, though its effects aren't truly seen until years later.

1966

The ISS' very own Vincent Price guest stars as the villain Egghead on the *Batman* television series. True to form, Price turns several crew members into wolf men.

1968

Supervillain puppet Richard Nixon is elected president of the United States.

1969

The whole world is fooled into thinking a man has walked on the moon for the first time. In fact, Neil Armstrong walked on a full-size replica moon the ISS placed just a few feet in front of the real moon. (Also, we had already been there many times.)

1973

A group of enterprising supervillains steals Japan and replaces it with a country full of crazy people who watch cartoons in which tentacle monsters rape women.

1974

Having exhausted his usefulness, Richard Nixon resigns as president under duress from his supervillain overlords, who had done all the damage they could do to hotels of a circular shape. Nixon is replaced by a mindless hologram named Gerald Ford.

1977

Supervillain mastermind George Lucas releases *Star Wars*, the greatest success in mass subliminal suggestion in history. (The suggestion: BUY MY SHIT.) The Psychomonitor is invented to measure its effects.

1979

The ISS stages the Iran hostage crisis to distract people while they construct their new nation-sized underground lair below Spain.

1981

The third supervillain president, Ronald Reagan, is sworn into office. His first unofficial act is to declare that all comics become "grim and gritty," ushering in the era of the "anti-hero."

1986

The Battle of the Underground Volcano Vortex results in the destruction of the League of Right Rightness, who had been severely weakened by the Grim and Gritty Act four years earlier. Greenland is also destroyed in the battle, though the ISS leads people to believe it still exists (for a future plan, the details of which cannot be divulged).

1987

With no arch-nemeses left to gum up the works, the ISS begins work on its 150-part World Domination Super-Plan.

1989

The Super-Plan is temporarily held up when all the ISS' members become obsessed to the point of distraction with a little group called Milli Vanilli.

1990

The revelation that Milli Vanilli had been lip-syncing their songs leads ISS leaders to attempt to recruit the duo as a reward for their incredible deception. The group's members, Rob and Fab, accept the offer, and commit supervillainy for several years under the name "Millain Vanillains."

1992

After the resolution of some infighting (with broken bones), work begins anew on the Super-Plan. Cars are made self-aware. Meanwhile, Great Britain's first and only supervillain prime minister, John Major, is re-elected using the power of his Hypno-Glasses.

1994

The ISS activates U2 singer Bono's Douchebag Matrix, inspiring a full generation of kids to be total douchebags.

1997

Master Lucas unleashes the special editions of his Star Wars films on the world so that the Psychomonitor can be improved and calibrated.

1999

Villains spread the false rumor that the Y2K bug could destroy the world's computer systems. This allows them to prepare for the Y2K8 bug, an old-fashioned plan that uses radio signals to cause people to default on their mortgages and destroy the world economy.

2001

Contrary to popular belief, supervillains had no involvement in the 9/11 attacks. But, because they are largely blamed for them, they have to go into hiding, again halting work on the Super-Plan and avoid airports. Several supervillains are victims of "evil profiling."

2005

Lord Lucas' final Star Wars film, *Revenge of the Sith*, is released. The Psychomonitor is perfected.

2007

The ISS begins step twenty-seven in its Super-Plan, creating the International Society of Supervillains website. Its creators are often bored, however, and end up writing a lot of off-topic stuff about pop culture, ice cream flavors and composer Aaron Copland.

2012

ISS co-founder King Oblivion, Ph.D., writes the group's how-to guide, a clever ruse, which causes its readers to . . .

Well, now you know, dear readers.

Villain Vocabulary: A Glossary for the Evil-doer

annihilate *(v.)* to destroy completely: *I annihilated this timeline using the AnnihiloClock, though by doing so, I also annihilated the Annihilo-Clock and myself.*

avarice *(n.)* the noble cause of greed.

bane *(n.)* 1. Something or someone that ruins or foils; a superhero; always followed by "my existence": *Mr. Wonderful is the bane of my existence.* 2. That guy who broke Batman's back; really has a lot of great stories if you get a couple beers in him

bow *(v.)* what you will eventually force everyone to do before you (see "kneel")

blast *(interj.)* what you say when you really mean, "shit!"

challenge *(v.)* call to fight or engage in other competition; *(n.)* the act of calling into competition; (Note: This word is only allowed in sentences containing the word "dare.")

childish *(adj.)* like a stupid baby who is dumb; anything a superhero does

command *(n.)* everything you say; *(v.)* what you will hopefully do for a living

cretinous *(adj.)* idiotic, henchman-like

crush *(v.)* to smash by squeezing; what you must constantly say you will do to anyone who opposes you

dare *(v.)* to act with heroic boldness or perhaps ignorant willfulness: *Foolish hero! You dare to enter my lair at 3:00 AM, when I have a really big day tomorrow?*

death ray *(n.)* a ray (see "ray") that causes death (not to be confused with a "hurt ray")

defile *(v.)* ruin or spoil; what superheroes regularly do to everything just by being around

demise *(n.)* a cool and dramatic way to say "death"

destroy *(v.)* sort of like "annihilate" or "crush;" this will be most of your day

dolt *(n.)* a stupid, henchmanesque person

doom *(n.)* the number-one goal

foil *(v.)* ruin or upend; what superheroes regularly do to plans: *Insolent fool! You have foiled my attempt to wrap the entire Pacific Ocean in aluminum foil!*

fool *(n.)* everyone who is not you (and, of course, me)

glorious *(adj.)* amazing; what it will be like when your plan finally comes to fruition

hamfisted *(adj.)* clumsy; used to describe any attempt by a superhero to do anything

hatred *(n.)* the driving force behind everything; the only emotion worth having

hurt ray *(n.)* does not exist

impending *(adj.)* coming; pretty much only goes with "doom" or "destruction"

indolent *(adj.)* slothful, like henchmen

ingenious *(adj.)* brilliant or clever; should be used to describe all of your plans

insolent *(adj.)* disobedient, like superheroes (and also henchmen)

justice *(n.)* revenge

kill *(v.)* temporarily incapacitate

kneel *(v.)* what you will eventually force everyone to do before you (see "bow")

lackey *(n.)* someone who is subservient; toady; often a cretinous dolt

laser *(n.)* sort of a ray, kind of (see "ray")

limitless *(adj.)* infinite; the only type of power worth fighting for

matter *(idiomatic)* "no matter," describing anything a superhero ever does

meddling *(v.)* also anything a superhero ever does

megalomaniacal *(adj.)* normal

minion *(n.)* smaller lackeys

pernicious *(adj.)* evil or wicked; used mainly for alliterative purposes

pilfer *(v.)* steal; used mainly for alliterative purposes

pusillanimous *(adj.)* cowardly; used mainly for alliterative purposes

power *(n.)* strength or level of control; useless if it is not limitless (see "limitless")

putrid *(adj.)* disgusting and foul; superheroish

ray *(n.)* sort of a laser, kind of (see "laser")

ray gun *(n.)* a gun that shoots rays of various kinds (contrary to a common misconception, can be used on people with names other than Ray)

relent *(v.)* to quit or slacken; what you will regularly command superheroes to do when you are pelting them with walking piranhas

reprobate *(n.)* a wicked or depraved person; for villains with skewed senses of justice, average people

repugnant *(adj.)* sickening or unattractive: *Having to watch you two teen heroes make out while I'm trying to fill the city reservoir with ghosts is repugnant!*

repulsive *(adj.)* repugnant: *Seriously! This is really damn repulsive! You know what? Fine! Take me to jail! If only to get away from you two!*

retreat *(v.)* run away from a fight; something you will constantly say you never do; something you will do all the time

revenge *(n.)* justice

ruse *(n.)* a trick, often carried out using disguises or other artifice; something superheroes somehow deal with by punching it away

sanctimonious *(adj.)* holier-than-thou; hypocritical; superheroes in a nutshell

sanctum *(n.)* lair or headquarters; place superheroes like to intrude upon with their sanctimoniousness

seductress *(n.)* a foxy lady who often fools superheroes into falling for a ruse; not really into me for some reason

submit *(v.)* what all will do in your presence!

surrender *(v.)* what you will occasionally do in their presence!

unmatched *(adj.)* without peer in terms of quality and power; how you should describe all of your plans

unstoppable *(adj.)* impossible to halt or end; how you should describe all of your plans

vengeance *(n.)* the act of achieving justice

vengeful *(adj.)* just; fair

vessel *(n.)* any vehicle you ride in or pilot: *Minions! Enter my vessel, this . . . pedicab!*

zap *(v.)* what you do to superheroes via ray guns; *(onomatopoeia)* the sound those ray guns make: *I will zap you now, do-gooder! [ZAP!]*

zounds *(interj.)* said when you are taken by surprise, which obviously will never happen